THE ROURKE CHRONICLES

VOLUME II

DEMONS AND MONSTERS

THE ROURKE CHRONICLES

VOLUME II

DEMONS AND MONSTERS

THE SURVIVALIST, John Thomas Rourke, from my perspective—
Paul Rubenstein.

With assistance from Jerry and Sharon Ahern and Bob Anderson. An
authorized companion series for Jerry Ahern's **THE SURVIVALIST**.

Jerry Ahern, Sharon Ahern and Bob Anderson

SPEAKING VOLUMES, LLC
NAPLES, FLORIDA
2017

THE ROURKE CHRONICLES
VOL II: DEMONS AND MONSTERS

Editing assistance provided by Pamela Anderson and Steve Servello.

ISBN 978-1-62815-817-5

DEDICATION

To John Robert and Shelley, my Michael and Annie, and to Mike Stadelmaier, who was my Paul Rubenstein.

To Sharon Ahern, a most remarkable woman, wife, mother and friend.

To Mike Spinnella, Steve Servello and James Morgan, my short stops, my guides and my standard bearers.

Without them this book would not have been possible.

Remember to Plan Ahead!

Bob

FOREWORD

Again, Jerry's entire family want to thank Paul Rubenstein for what must have been a long and difficult undertaking, to continue the retelling of the life and times of the Rourke family. What it must have been like to go back and relive this terrible period known forever as The Night of the War. Paul suffered through the agony of uncalculated loss of life and the horror of a world gone mad not once, but once again, so that our world will hopefully not go down that same path.

Through the reading of Jerry's interviews with John Thomas Rourke, Paul was not only able to relate his recollections of this time in our past but also give us a greater sense of the people affected by this brief conflict. There were many heroes who rose up to meet the challenge and there were many who sank into the mire, intent only on evil. Paul gives us a glimpse of both the good and the wicked and all those souls crammed in the middle, but more importantly, he shows us that the will to survive is strong in us all.

Most of us are well aware that our tenure on this mound of earth and sky and sea will not be nearly as lengthy as that allotted to the Rourkes. Perhaps now would be a good time to plan ahead and decide on our own course of action before we reach time's boundaries.

Sharon Ahern

INTRODUCTION

In the first volume of The Rourke Chronicles, I acknowledged I have given up trying to count the number of times I started this book. It actually began shortly after our initial meeting, a meeting I will never forget. In that instant I went from a quiet journalist, and semi-practicing Jewish boy, to a man, thrust into a world I never conceived of.

Recent archaeological finds at the former Museum of Natural History in Chicago, the former Cheyenne Mountain complex, several sites in Texas, as well as interviews with members of the Rourke family have been used to tell this story.

I continue to use one of the most faithful accounts to supplement my efforts, the works of John Thomas Rourke's friend, Jerry. Since Jerry's passing, his estate and his family have given permission to use his material.

Paul Rubenstein

PART ONE
WE FOUND THE SAVAGE HORDE

CHAPTER ONE

Natalia Anastasia Tiemerovna, Major, KGB and I had hooked up with some Free American Force troopers to search for John Thomas Rourke. We carried an urgent message for him from her uncle, General Ishmael Varakov, the leader of the Soviet Occupation Forces in America. A man who many times had shown himself to be a patriotic, honorable and reasonable soldier; even if he was a Russian.

We feared Rourke had not survived the massive storms which had swept the coast and central section of the country.

Suddenly, over the roar of our Harley motorcycles we heard gunfire ahead. Our troopers stopped their military pickup truck; Natalia and I split up and proceeded on foot while they provided cover.

I came up through the trees behind Natalia and off to her right. A man's form lay on the ground at the edge of the trees; unmoving. She unsnapped the flaps of the Safariland holsters on her hips. The two customized, slab-side barreled stainless L-Frames leapt into her hands, muzzles leveled at the tree line as she walked and I covered her with the Schmeisser.

My attention was divided between watching her and covering the woods around us. Five yards from the man's form she stopped. Glancing from side to side, she walked forward while I searched the trees for a trap.

Natalia stopped beside the body, kicking it once in the exposed rib cage just to be sure, then she stepped back quickly. The man lay still; dead.

Holstering the revolver in her left hand, she dropped to her knees, touching the dead man's cheek. "Still warm," she murmured. "Two bullet holes in the body..."

Standing up, she walked in the direction she judged the shots had been fired. She stooped to the ground and picked up a piece of shiny brass, a freshly fired .45 ACP cartridge.

Natalia glanced at the head stamp. "Hmm," she murmured. There was a second cartridge case and she picked it up; "Identical."

A disturbance in the leaves a few feet further on, she walked toward it, the imprint of motorcycle tracks. She studied the tracks. "John?"

She bent over, taking a dry leaf and touching it to the glistening, moist leaves. Without bringing it too close to her nose, she sniffed. "Urine. Probably human." There was another, similar wet spot few feet to the left.

I spotted something on the ground near me, partially obscured by leaves. Picking it up, I jogged toward Natalia, my Schmeisser submachine gun dangling from its sling under my right arm. I held up the disassembled parts of a riot shotgun. "I found this, somebody deliberately made it inoperable."

She nodded, "It can still function, single shot, if you hand chamber the rounds. I think John was here, Paul, and not too long ago; maybe just a few minutes ago."

"The loud shot we heard was from this?" I asked, indicating the shotgun.

She nodded and opened her hand. "And the two lighter ones from these," showing me the spent cartridge cases.

I took them from her, inspecting them. I checked the head stamp; it was the ammo brand that John Thomas Rourke carried, but it was also what she carried. "That's John's brand all right."

"There are motorcycle tracks and someone urinated here about the time we heard the shots. That dead man's flesh is still warm. I think it was John, stopped to... to..."

"To piss," I nodded, smiling embarrassedly.

Natalia smiled. "Yes, and somebody came up on him, that man over there. John shot him, disassembled his shotgun so no one could use it afterward, then, finished pissing and drove off."

"But when there's one brigand, there's usually a bunch of 'em," I said.

"Did you find any signs of more?" Natalia asked.

3

"Nothing, no," I shook my head, my left hand pushing my wire rimmed glasses up off the bridge of my nose.

"Neither did I. If you were John..."

I laughed. "Ha, if I were John... If anybody is closer to John in the way they think, it is you. What would you do, kill one brigand and figure there are more around?"

She thought then said, "John urinated twice, as if he'd been doing it when he heard the man. After he killed him, John checked the man's pockets. I noticed they were turned inside out when I checked the body. Then John finished what he'd been doing."

"That's John for you," I smiled. "He would have waited here long enough to tell if others were coming, and none did. This guy could have been a straggler."

She said, "There wasn't any bike, no signs of a truck or anything so he could have been alone and on foot."

I shook my head. "I don't think so."

"Me either," she said. "The soles of his boots are polished almost smooth, but they weren't worn down as if he'd walked a great deal."

I said, "John would have figured there were brigands in the area and whatever they were doing, hearing what maybe would have been gunshots wasn't important enough to pull them away."

Natalia nodded. "Laying a trap..."

She touched her left hand gently to my right forearm. "John is probably looking for the other brigands, the rest of the dead man's gang."

"Can't be more than a couple miles, guy wouldn't have left his wheels."

"He could have been a scout, maybe from a base camp. But you're right, Paul. Not more than a few miles."

"If we can back track him through the woods..." I started.

"We'll know soon enough if John did the same thing," she interrupted. "And we can find him..."

"Before he runs into a dozen or two brigands I hope," I added soberly.

"Before... yes. Come on," and she started running back toward her bike. I threw the useless shotgun into the trees as I ran for my bike and signaled our troopers to follow.

She reached her own machine, snapped closed the flaps of the Safariland holsters for the stainless Smith & Wessons on her hips, straddled the machine and brought the engine to life.

*****

My Reflection:

This was actually one of my most favorite times. Being alone with Natalia... it is hard to describe, but by this time I realized my infatuation with, and for her, had grown into love. It was a love that would never be mine to complete... only to treasure. She belonged to someone else, my best friend. But, my word... she was, and still is, gorgeous!

CHAPTER TWO

I heard gunfire ahead of us and slowed my bike; Natalia pulled up alongside of me.

"Must be John," I shouted, working open the bolt of the Schmeisser with my left hand and giving the Browning High Power a good luck tug in the tanker style shoulder holster across my chest.

Natalia said nothing but she pulled back the bolt of her M-16. The rifle was slung crossbody, as Rourke carried his.

"Let's go," I said.

"We'll split when we reach the battle site, you take the right flank, I'll take the left," she answered. We sent the troopers around to the left along the road and I revved my machine, punched out, jerking the fork wildly as I dodged tree trunks. The gunfire was louder now, heavy automatic weapons fire like I'd heard so many times before in the weeks since I first met John Rourke; in the weeks since the Night of The War.

The ground evened out, I jerked the Harley hard right, almost losing it. I bent low now, building RPMs as I sped the machine along the crest of the rise. There was a forested area a hundred yards ahead, the gunfire was coming from just beyond it, heavier even than it had been. "I'll head through the trees; you go around 'em, Natalia!" I shouted.

"Yes, Paul!" I heard her call back, not looking. That she obeyed my instructions without hesitation amused me for an instant. "Yes, Paul," I laughed to myself.

I bent lower over the machine, thorns and pine boughs swatted at my face and exposed hands, slapping against my olive drab field jacket. I saw movement in the trees to the far left, a man, running, firing an assault rifle.

I slowed the bike, the rear tire spraying dirt and pine needles. I hit the kill switch and let the bike drop and ran into the trees.

The man turned... the assault rifle to his shoulder ready to fire. I swung the Schmeisser forward on its sling, then stopped.

It was John Rourke. I couldn't help myself, I let out a yell; my counterfeit rebel yell complete with a New York accent.

Rourke broke into a smile. "Paul, over here; keep down!" Rourke wheeled, ducking down himself, a fusillade of automatic weapons fire poured toward him, hammering into the trees surrounding him.

I returned fire with the Schmeisser as John pumped the CAR-15's trigger, edging back into the trees. I saw a flicker of movement at the base of the hill, along the near edge of the valley. Dark hair blew back straight from the neck, dark clothes, an M-16 firing.

"Natalia!" Rourke shouted the name.

Gunfire was pouring toward her on the bike now. She turned the bike hard right toward the base of the hill, then skidding in the dirt. She leapt from the machine to the cover of rocks.

I lost sight of her for an instant, then saw the flash from her rifle, heard the long burst aimed toward the hillside. She was coming to our rescue.

Rourke glanced behind him, I was nearly up alongside him as he rammed a fresh thirty-round magazine up the CAR-l5's well. Then he started to run, shouting to me, "Paul, give that rebel yell of yours!"

I did and let loose half of a magazine of 9mm rounds just to keep our enemies busy.

Natalia's M-16 poured into the brigands, and at last our six troopers began to maneuver forward, their M-16s blazing. The nearest brigands perhaps thirty yards away now.

As I changed mags in the Schmeisser, I saw Rourke fire out the CAR-15 and snatch the twin stainless Detonics pistols from the shoulder rig under his jacket, letting the CAR-15 drop to his side on its sling.

He fired both .45s simultaneously, the 185-grain JHPs thudding into the face of the nearest brigand; the man's body hurtling back, the head seeming to explode; blood, almost like a cloud, momentarily filling the air.

The military troopers with us were closing now. Those brigands who remained alive were trapped and because of that, more dangerous than before.

I lost sight of Rourke as two brigands came at him in a rush. A third was launching himself at me with a knife in one hand.

I swung the Schmeisser like a bat, the front sight opening a gash in the man's face that ran from his left ear, across the cheek and slicing through his left eye socket.

The man screamed; I jerked the Schmeisser's buttstock back and squeezed the trigger hard.

I had learned to fire single shots with a controlled trigger pull, but the only mode of fire for the Schmeisser is fully automatic. Right now my adrenalin was flowing like a river and before I released the trigger I had almost cut the man in half.

I looked back and saw Rourke throw himself down, firing at an upward angle toward the man with the assault rifle. The man's body doubled over, toppling forward, the 5.56 mms spraying a steady stream into the ground at the already dead, still falling man's feet.

Rourke rolled, trying to acquire the second target, the one with a revolver.

I heard the burst of Rourke's automatic weapon fire, and the revolver's roar. At the same time I squeezed a short burst from the Schmeisser, saw the man's body fall and swung back to engage another attacker coming at me.

Rourke shouted, "Paul, thanks!" I was still firing but I couldn't see Natalia through the trees and gun smoke. Then I saw Natalia's gleaming custom revolvers belch bright bursts of fire, men falling before her.

I was firing the Schmeisser with my right hand and the battered Browning High Power in my left.

*****

The last of the brigand bodies now lay on the ground, twitching, nerves firing even in death. Natalia stood, the matched Smiths limp in her hands.

The slide was locked back and open on the emptied Browning. I reloaded and shoved it into my belt. I dropped the Schmeisser, letting it dangle at my side. I stood quietly, my right hand held my glasses; I closed my eyes.

Rourke let out a long, hard breath, a sigh. I saw him take a cigar from his pocket and light the thin, dark tobacco in the blue-yellow flame of the Zippo which bore his initials. He smiled and inhaled the smoke deep into his lungs.

Had we been unskilled at fighting we would have been dead.

CHAPTER THREE

We reloaded our weapons and rechecked the brigands' bodies; all dead, as our entourage of troopers came up.

"So, Dr. Rourke, we came looking for you. That's why we're here. President Chambers and Colonel Reed..."

Rourke looked up from loading the six-round Detonics magazine. "Colonel Reed?"

"President Chambers personally promoted him, Sir." Rourke nodded and then looked back to the magazine. I slid the Browning into the shoulder holster.

Rourke picked up the Detonics and jacked back the slide, locking it with the slide stop. "So you're Captain Cole..."

"That's right, Sir. Regis Cole, recently promoted myself," and the young, green-eyed man smiled.

"Hmmm," Rourke said as he nodded.

I had estimated Cole's age at perhaps twenty-five, the five enlisted men with him younger still. Rourke inserted the magazine up the Detonics' well and gave it a pat on the butt, reassuring himself that it was seated, then worked the slide stop downward, the slide running forward, stripping the first round. Rourke started to lower the hammer.

"I always carry my .45 with the magazine completely full and a round in the chamber," Cole noted.

Rourke smiled. "A lot of people do," Rourke almost whispered, inhaling on the cigar in the left corner of his mouth. "But a lot of professional gunmen advocate or advocated, I guess these days, stripping the round for the chamber off the top of the magazine."

"To relieve spring pressure?"

"It helps, but not for that," and Rourke thumbed out the magazine with the release button. "Here," he pointed to the top round in the magazine. "Notice how it's edged forward just a little. Makes for more positive feeding than starting with a magazine where the top round has the case head all the way back against the spine of the magazine."

"Anyway, always works for me," and Rourke replaced the magazine in the pistol and began securing the Detonics under his left armpit in the holster there. He looked over at me and winked. "Why were you looking for me, anyway? What'd Reed want?"

Cole squatted on the ground beside Rourke and slightly at an angle to him, looked around, then behind him.

"I'd rather, ahh... talk a bit more privately, Dr. Rourke," Cole said hoarsely.

"There's nothing I wouldn't trust Paul or Natalia with..."

"She's a Russian, Sir. I must insist, Sir," Cole said again.

Rourke nodded and then a little louder than he needed said, "Natalia, Paul! The captain's going to tell me something in private. I'll tell you all about it as soon as he's through."

Rourke stood up; Cole's green eyes were icy. "Satisfy you?" Rourke smiled.

"I can impress you into service, Dr. Rourke, and then you'll have to do as I say."

"Draft me?" Rourke laughed, spontaneously picking up his CAR-15, the magazines for the weapon reloaded from ammo scrounged from the dead brigands. "You can't draft me."

Rourke started walking off toward the tree line, Cole beside him. The air was tense for some reason and as the rest of the U.S. military personnel closed in, I stuck a fresh magazine into the Schmeisser, just in case.

Suddenly, John wheeled, the Detonics pistols coming into his fists as he dropped into a crouch. The clicking of M-16 bolts mixed with the sound of rattling steel as the bolt of my Schmeisser opened.

11

Cole had a Government Model 1911A1 half out of the leather, letting it roll out of his hand on the trigger guard.

"You put your gun away, or I'll kill you," Rourke hissed at him. "And tell your own people to put their rifles down or you'll be the first to die."

"At least let me explain."

"You wanna explain, I'll be down there, with my friends. You tell me, you tell them."

Cole said nothing for a moment; then he only nodded. Holstering his pistol, he shouted loudly, "As you were!"

Rourke pointed the pistols in his balled, tightened fists toward the ground; then lowered the hammers with his thumbs.

John turned his back to the Army captain and started down the hillside again. I kept the Schmeisser ready. Cole continued, "... that nobody else could do the job. Your country needs you, Dr. Rourke."

Rourke stopped walking. "What job is it that no one else can do?" Rourke spit out the stump of burned, chewed cigar butt, then looked Cole in the eye.

"During a debriefing session, you mentioned to Colonel Reed that you had known Colonel Armand Teal before the war..."

"We shared an igloo together for three nights on an Arctic survival exercise. I know him."

"He's the commanding officer of Filmore Air Force Base in Northern California..."

"Hope he can swim," Rourke said soberly.

"We've determined that Filmore survived. It was well above the fault line and the mountain chain there would have protected it from the tidal wave effects when the San Andreas went. And there were only neutron hits there as far as we can ascertain over flights. There even seemed to be some activity, a U.S. flag flying."

"Could be the Russians," Rourke said.

"Sure, but we've tried contacting the base. Interference, static... we can't get through and no one answered when the reconnaissance over flight tried radio contact. If it had been the Commies, they would have answered."

"What's so important about Filmore Air Force Base and Armand Teal, you want me to tell you about him?"

"We want you to talk with him." Cole smiled.

"Go to California? Bullshit!" and Rourke turned and started walking back down the hillside, Natalia walking beside him.

She had told me she was going to let Rourke know that her uncle, General Ishmael Varakov, had sent a note to Rourke requesting an "immediate" meeting on a matter of "grave importance" not only for the world but for the Rourke family.

She was also going to tell him that as much as she loved and wanted him, more than anything else she wanted him to find Sarah and the children. Even if that meant there was no place for her. I figured she had accomplished both missions because when I saw her face again... tears were running down her cheeks.

CHAPTER FOUR

The trouble started about twenty minutes later. I saw it start and shouted, "John!"

Rourke picked up the CAR-15 from the sling where it hung, starting to run. He stopped on the top of the rise.

Natalia and Cole were faced off, Cole reaching out to slap Natalia. Her reflexes took over, catching the hand at the wrist, her body twisting as she side-stepped.

Cole was sailing up and forward; rolling over, crashing down onto his back. An assault rifle discharged as Natalia started settling her hands on her hips, too close to the twin stainless .357 Magnums she wore there.

Natalia spun around, both pistols still in the leather, her hands clutching at her abdomen. "John..." It was like a wail as she sprawled forward.

"Natalia!"

He and I were running, my Schmeisser covering the six soldiers and Cole. "Freeze, nobody move," I shouted.

"Natalia!" Rourke screamed again. "Natalia!" Her body was writhing on the ground as I ran past Cole. He moved faster than I thought he could. The pistol he'd pulled twenty minutes earlier coming from the leather again, the base of the frame this time smashing down on my arm carrying the Schmeisser.

I half-wheeled. My hand was limp from the impact, but I still tried to get Cole's throat. My Schmeisser forgotten as rage drove me.

"Get him, alive!" It was Cole's voice.

Rourke wheeled, his CAR-15 coming up, firing a three round semi-auto burst with the CAR-15. Cole spun, falling back.

Rourke kept going, toward Natalia. I heard the working of the bolts and saw the four M-16 muzzles rise. Rourke stopped, his rifle up and on line with them. "I'm going to the woman, if you try to stop me, I'll kill you."

Rourke started ahead, pushing the muzzles of the rifles aside. He didn't care to look at the men behind him. The man who had shot Natalia simply stood beside her, his right foot kicking out to check if she were dead.

Rourke snapped the telescoped butt of the CAR-15 up and out. His body wheeled with it, the metal buttplate at the end of the tubular stock hammering square into the soldier's face.

Rourke's right knee smashed up, finding the groin, impacting against the scrotum, the man's bloodied face going white as he fell.

"The woman," Rourke rasped. "Or your deaths." Rourke dropped to his knees beside her, her fingers covering her abdomen, blood seeping through between them as he rolled her over. The eyelids fluttered.

"Rourke, Rourke." It was Cole. "Rourke, you fuckin' shot me!"

Rourke began to examine the wound. Had he not been a physician, never seen a gunshot wound, had he never seen death... he must recognize it now in her face. Hell, I could see it.

That was when Cole struck. Intent as I had been on watching John work on Natalia, Cole had cold cocked me before I saw it coming. Cole shouted, "You're going with me Rourke, for those six missiles; eighty megatons apiece, Rourke. Eighty megatons apiece; the woman's good as dead. You want your Jew friend dead too?"

Rourke looked up for an instant, his eyes flickering across the field toward Cole. Cole's left arm bloodied and limp at his side, but in the right hand the Government Model .45 held steady, the muzzle pointed at my head as I struggled to get up.

"Where's your base camp, Cole? How do you contact headquarters?" Rourke began examining Natalia's wound in greater detail, spreading her fingers, but slowly.

I wondered, were her hands holding in her intestines? Gently, he broke the tight weave of her red and sticky fingers. "Where is it?"

15

"A submarine, two hours away, maybe three. Nuclear submarine, one of the last ones we could contact. Full complement crew, full medical facilities."

Behind John came a moan from the trooper who had shot Natalia and then kicked her. Rourke had smashed in his face with the rifle butt, broken his nose and twisted it to one side of his face; his lips puffed and gushing blood.

"We keep our guns, we get Natalia the best medical attention available," Rourke called out over his shoulder, his voice low.

"Agreed," Cole snapped. "Then you're coming to Filmore Air Force Base..."

He shook his head, "I didn't say that."

He made it clear we had to get her to the submarine and treat the bullets in Cole's arm and the wounded trooper here.

"Paul." John called my name but never looked up. "Get on your feet and keep that thing you call a Schmeisser handy. Anything happens to Natalia..." He let the sentence hang.

My voice was low and angry, "Killing would be too good." I raked the bolt back and waited.

I walked to the two of them. Glancing down I asked in a whisper, "What do you think, John?" I could see her exposed intestines, almost gray in color, like pieces of undercooked sausage in appearance.

He never looked up or answered me. As he tightened the pressure bandage, I could hear him pray for God to let him get her to the medical facilities. Then he would operate and he asked God not to let her die.

*****

My Reflection:

It took a while for the submarine to arrive and it seemed even longer for us to explain the situation and get Natalia on board. John stayed focused on her care; I stayed focused on Cole... God forgive me; I really wanted to kill that man.

CHAPTER FIVE

Inside the submarine, I stood behind Natalia's gurney while John continued to work on her. There was whole blood available and while hers was being typed, he was coordinating with the ship's doctor on transfusions for Natalia and the injured trooper.

Rourke motioned for me. "Get the nurse to take a look at the knot Cole put on your head. Then I need you to get some rest. I want one of us with Natalia at all times."

"But..." I started to object but was cut off by the look on John's face. I think it was then I really got scared. Natalia might die; it was no longer an academic possibility. It was a fact. I stepped away from the gurney and drew the curtain behind me.

I walked down the passage way, I could smell coffee. I poured a cup and sat down. I noticed my hands were shaking. I sat the coffee cup down.

CHAPTER SIX

My scalp wound was cleaned; eight stitches closed the "hole in my head." X-rays were taken, no skull fracture... not even a concussion. *Then why does my head hurt so badly?*

I walked back toward the medical bay and leaned against the wall—excuse me—the bulkhead and listened.

I could hear the ship's doctor, "Doctor Rourke, we typed her at O Positive; lucky for her it wasn't a negative RH factor. I'm getting as many five hundred milliliter size transfusion bags made up as I can."

"You've got filters for clot removal?" Rourke asked automatically.

"Yes, we're getting the tubing ready for her now."

Rourke said, "Let's start those transfusion bags, her pressure is falling and it's falling too fast."

That was all I could take. I walked back toward the coffee pot. This time I noticed a small sign on the bulkhead. It said, "Officer's Mess."

*****

My Reflection:

I had been scared almost since the plane crashed and the Night of the War... however, it was during this time when Natalia was so terribly injured that I felt true panic. I didn't know what John Rourke would have done if she had died; the woman he loved...

I didn't know what I would have done either, since I loved her as well.

CHAPTER SEVEN

I was nursing yet another cup of coffee when an older man came in the Officer's Mess, poured a cup of coffee and sat down across from me. "What's the name of this boat anyway?" I asked.

"Well, Mr. Rubenstein, you've got the terminology right. We call her a boat. I guess calling her a 'her' is kinda dumb, but it's tradition. She's the U.S.S. John Paul Jones."

"How'd you know my name?" I looked at the radiation badge I'd been given as soon as I'd come aboard. No name appeared on it.

"My business to know everything that goes on aboard this boat." The man said extending his hand, "I'm Bob Gundersen, Commander Gundersen, sort of an affectionate title the men use with me. Sometimes they just call me Captain, though."

I took the hand; it was warm, dry, solid. "My friends call me Paul, Commander."

"Paul, it is then."

"If you know everything that goes on this ship, then tell me how Natalia's doing." I wished again I'd not given up smoking years earlier.

"Major Tiemerovna?" He glanced at his watch, a Rolex like Rourke wore. "Dr. Rourke started transfusing blood into her about ten minutes ago. He may be operating by now, I don't know."

"I wish John weren't."

"Doctor Rourke?"

"Yeah, John; I wish he wasn't operating. I remember reading something once that doctors aren't supposed to operate on family members; people they're close to; too much of a stress situation."

"I asked Doctor Rourke the same thing myself," Gundersen said as he nodded, sipping at his coffee. "He said he'd checked with our doctor, but our Doctor Milton has never worked on a gunshot wound before. He's fresh out of medical school two years ago.

"Before the Night of The War at least, we didn't have many gunshot wounds in the Navy. Now, of course, we don't really have a Navy at all. All the surface ships are gone or at least gone out of contact. Not many of us in the pigboat fleet left either."

"Pigboats?"

"Old submariner's term, real old; but I'm an old submariner." Gundersen smiled. "Guess that's why it doesn't bother me to use it. Anyway, Dr. Milton never had worked on gunshot wounds before and your friend Doctor Rourke said this one was bad.

"Guess there wasn't much choice. I bumped into Milton outside the sick bay just before Rourke began transfusing Major Tiemerovna. Milton seemed to think Rourke was good. I just hope Harvey was right."

"Brought this along, figured you might be needing it. Sometimes the waiting gets harder than the doing." From the seat beside him Gundersen produced a small slab-sided bottle.

He smiled, "Medicinal liquor, I've drunk smoother, but there's more where it comes from," and Gundersen handed me the bottle.

I downed my coffee, twisted open the bottle and poured two fingers into the cup. I offered the bottle to Gundersen. "Never touch the stuff when we're underway."

"What's that mean?"

"We've been underwater and heading north for..." he looked at his wristwatch. "Fifty-eight minutes. They don't really need me up there until we get near the icepack, and that'll be a while yet. Should be tricky; imagine there's been a lot of shifting in the pack since the Night of the War."

"Icepack?" I asked and coughed, the medicinal liquor was strong, burning as I felt it in the pit of my stomach.

"As to the running of the submarine here and the welfare of my crew, I give the orders. But for the actual operation, its Captain Cole's say so. He ordered us underway before they put him out to take out the two slugs in his left arm."

CHAPTER EIGHT

I sat with Commander Gundersen for some time. It would be quite a while before I would find out what was happening during Natalia's surgery. What I did know was it was taking, at least in my opinion, an incredibly long time. Something had to be wrong.

Something had complicated an already complicated surgery. John Rourke was dealing with... God knows what. It was his job to save Natalia's life and right now he probably had her very life literally in his hands.

I reached for another dose of medicinal alcohol, but stopped. I realized while I would have loved an alcohol fog to ease my fears, I had no desire to get drunk. No, not accurate... I did want to get drunk but I couldn't.

*****

Six hours had passed since her surgery began. If I felt such torture waiting for the outcome of the operation, I could not even imagine what it was like for John Rourke.

A slip of the scalpel, a misjudgment and a woman that Rourke obviously loved would be dead. I shivered, not from cold.

A voice from behind said, "The operation's over." It was Rourke.

I jerked around. She was dead, I thought. "John, is..."

"She should make it," Rourke said shaking his head. His face was haggard looking. Somehow leaner seeming than I had ever seen it.

Even under the most bizarre conditions, I had secretly marveled that Rourke always found the time to stay clean shaven when there was sufficient water available to do so. But now, his face was stubbled, deep lines etched there heightened by the shadow of beard.

"You look like hell," I said quietly.

Rourke nodded, "Matches the way I feel..." The last slug fragmented, he had to reconstruct it under a microscope.

"What are we going to do, John?"

"If I got everything and did everything right, Natalia could be up and around in about a week. We can't do anything until then. You meet the captain?"

"Commander Gundersen, yeah, seems okay."

"It's Cole we've gotta worry about, those orders of his, something doesn't sound right about them."

I said, "He acts like he wants to start a nuclear war all over again? That's crazy."

Rourke rubbed his chin, absently, "I'm going to see if there's some way this Commander Gundersen can contact President Chambers or Reed. But in the meantime, we're stuck."

"Gundersen's men took my guns, I didn't see any way of arguing it, six of them and no running room."

Rourke nodded soberly. "I took off my pistols when I scrubbed, most of them anyway," and Rourke smiled. "But you were right; trying a shootout in a metal skin in the water... under it now, would have been stupid."

"You're not going through with this, to find the missiles. Are you?"

Rourke frowned. "I don't have much choice. We'll be there anyway when this thing surfaces, and if I can contact Chambers and he confirms that Cole is acting on his behalf, then I'll have to. But, my gut still tells me there's something wrong, really wrong with Cole and his outfit."

"What if Cole is some kind of crazy, or maybe a Russian Natalia wouldn't have known about, or something else. We can't let him get his hands on those six missiles. There is an eighty megaton capacity for each missile; nearly five hundred megatons combined."

Rourke sat down holding his head in his hands for a moment, then looked up. He picked up the bottle of medicinal liquor. "Looks like it tastes great..."

"You'll get used to it," I said with a smile.

Rourke said nothing else, reaching into his shirt pocket and taking one of the dark tobacco cigars and lighting it, his face more lined and tired than before.

CHAPTER NINE

"John! John!"

"Damnit!" Rourke sat straight up and then opened his eyes, light in a yellow shaft coming through from the companionway as I shook him awake. "What's the matter?"

"Doctor Milton says Natalia's dying." Rourke pushed himself from the cot and started into the companionway. I ran beside him.

CHAPTER TEN

Milton had arranged for men who had volunteered to donate a second pint of blood. I stood in line with them, checking my watch. Slowly, the line moved. Maybe it was moving at the exact correct speed; I didn't know but it seemed it was moving slowly. Finally, it was my turn.

"Any word?" I asked.

The pharmacist mate shook his head. "Nothing I have heard but we're still asking for more volunteers. That means she is losing a lot of blood. About all I can tell you. Squeeze this." He gave me a tennis ball, thumbed my elbow looking for a vein and inserted the needle.

He pulled the needle out, stuck a cotton wad on the wound and taped it down. I sat up and he handed me a small bottle of orange juice. "Drink this and take it easy for a few hours."

I glanced at my watch. Over eighty minutes had ticked off since the second operation started.

I heard a hatch open and turned, Rourke stepped in, blood half way up his forearms, staining his gown, his gloved hands splotched with it, her blood. He stripped away the gloves and stuffed them in the pocket of the surgical gown he had taken off. In his hand was a single bullet.

"Got you, you bastard." He swore at it then dropped it in his pocket.

CHAPTER ELEVEN

I had lost all sense of day and night. When I awoke it took a moment before I remembered we were on a nuclear submarine. Then my thoughts began to bounce around.

Were Sarah and the children somewhere in Georgia or the Carolinas or Alabama or Mississippi or even in Tennessee?

Then I thought about Natalia and how close she had come to dying.

I showered and shaved and met Rourke in the Officer's Mess over coffee where he gave me a Reader's Digest version of a conversation with Gundersen.

"What did Gundersen want?"

Rourke shook his head. "I'm not sure he really wanted anything but to talk. We talked about Natalia, he was genuinely concerned. Then we went to his cabin for a private talk."

"Did you discuss Cole?"

Rourke smiled. "Yeah and Gundersen doesn't have any better opinion of him than we do. He did make contact with President Chambers and Colonel Reed, or thinks he did... but this was all over the radio. Reed advised him they were sending Cole and a small patrol for an urgent mission that Gundersen could help with."

"This urgent mission the one Cole told us about?"

"Yeah, find Fremont Air Base, the sub gets us as close as it can. We go in and retrieve the warheads and get them back to the sub then deliver them to U.S. II Headquarters or wherever; that last part hasn't been spelled out yet."

"What does Gundersen say about Cole?"

Rourke grinned. "Called him a prick but says he has the President's signature on his written orders. But he still doesn't trust him. Gundersen said he disarmed you and me to keep the peace but will rearm us when we surface. He has promised to keep Natalia safe and I believe him."

Rourke presented a black leather pouch snapped closed with a brass fitting. "He gave me this."

Inside were six Detonics stainless magazines, the magazines empty as Rourke looked more closely, the magazines ranked side by side, floor plates up.

"It is called a 'Six Pack', Milt Sparks made 'em before the Night of The War. Mostly they were for Government Models, but Gundersen had this one made for his Detonics CombatMaster. He lost the pistol overboard and had no more use for it so he gave it to me."

*****

My Reflection:

From that day to this, I have lost count of the number of times John carried the Milt Sparks Six Pack. It became as much a part of the Rourke legend as the Alessi double shoulder holster.

CHAPTER TWELVE

John Rourke told me later that he was watching Natalia sleep when her eyelids fluttered. "She was climbing out of the darkness and trying to awaken. I stood up, walked to her bed and touched her left shoulder," he said.

"Her eyes opened; the brilliance of the blue somehow deeper in the gray light of the room. A smile tracked on her lips, her voice odd sounding. She whispered 'I love you,' then closed her eyes. I stood beside the bed for a long time."

CHAPTER THIRTEEN

Days later, John, Natalia and I sat, our eyes transfixed on the television monitors in the crew mess. All of the sub's complement that was not on duty watched the screens as we viewed the devastation in another city.

Earlier we had passed the ruins of San Francisco, a city where once people lived... now an underwater tomb.

A young seaman first class had been born in the city we were passing. He had lived there; his mother, father, two sisters, wife and infant son had died there.

Someone started to change the image on the monitor but the young seaman had insisted on watching, and now he wept.

Natalia, wearing a robe borrowed from the captain, moving slowly, her left hand holding her abdomen where Rourke had made the incisions, stood.

Rourke started up after her, but she shook her head, murmuring, "No, John," then she walked. Supporting herself against the long, spotlessly clean tables, she moved to the side of the weeping man.

"I am sorry, for your family and you," she whispered.

The young man looked up. "Why'd you and your people wanna kill us, we coulda talked it out, or somethin'?"

"I don't know, sailor, I don't know," she whispered. He looked at her, just shaking his head.

She moved her hands, touching them lightly to his shoulders. He looked down, his neck bent, his shoulders slumping. Natalia took a step toward him, leaning against him to help herself stand, her arms folding around his neck, his head coming to rest against her abdomen.

She closed her eyes as he wept. John and I looked at each other... neither of us had words or ideas of how to make things better.

CHAPTER FOURTEEN

It was crowded and cold as we stood in the sail of the submarine. Thick, large snowflakes fell, the temperature barely cold enough for them. Natalia Anastasia Tiemerovna shivered beside John and he folded his arm around her to give her warmth.

The submarine was moving through the fjord-like cut in the land and toward the new coastline. We were at what had been north central California. Beneath the wake, the sub's prow cut were the bodies of the dead and cities they had lived in.

There was a bay that had been carved at the far end of the inlet. Commander Gundersen on the sail beside us was in constant radio contact with his bridge for depth soundings of the fjord. It had been created by the mega quakes that had destroyed California beyond the San Andreas Fault line on the Night of the War.

There were no charts.

"I'm running even at eighteen feet below the water," Gundersen looked away, snapping into the handset. "Wilkins, this is it, we get ourselves hung up bad enough, we can't dive. All stop. Then give me the most accurate soundings you can all through the bay. I want a channel I can stay over where I can dive if I have to. Once you've got that, feed in the coordinates and back her up, you got the con."

"Aye, Captain," the voice rattled back.

Gundersen put down the set. "You've been avoiding Captain Cole."

John nodded, saying, "You said you didn't want a fight on board ship."

"Well, let's all get below and talk this out so we know what the hell we're doing, huh?" Gundersen didn't wait for an answer; but retrieved the handset, depressing the push-to-talk button.

"Wilkins, Gundersen. Get Captain Cole sent over to my cabin in about three minutes."

"Aye, Skipper."

Gundersen started below, cautioning. "Watch your step, miss," to Natalia. She nodded, starting down the hatchway after him.

I caught at Rourke's arm. "We really gonna go through with this?"

"Cole wants those warheads, whether he's just carrying out his orders or for some other reason. Only way we can know is to be there with him when he gets them."

I nodded. "I was afraid you were gonna say that."

John smiled. "Come on, watch your step. Slippery…"

I nodded as Rourke looked away, there was more to watch your step about than ice on the sail.

CHAPTER FIFTEEN

"I need Doctor Rourke with me, Rubenstein can stay here. And no guns for Rourke," Cole said flatly.

Gundersen wove the fingers of his hands together. "I anticipated that, Captain Cole. I've talked briefly here with Doctor Rourke. Sending a man out unarmed into what might be out there would be like committing murder. Doctor Rourke gets his guns..."

"I object to that, Sir!"

"I'll note that objection in my log." Gundersen went on placidly as Rourke and I watched his eyes. "And as to Mr. Rubenstein, he chooses to accompany his friend and he certainly may. Lieutenant O'Neal, my missile officer hasn't had much to do since we fired all our missiles you know, so, he's coming along as well as are a few of my men on the landing party.

"Lieutenant O'Neal can be responsible for Mr. Rubenstein if that suits you better. And as to Major Tiemerovna, there's no policy decision to be made there. She's not strong enough yet to travel. So she doesn't need her guns. Questions about that, Captain?"

"I still protest, Sir, once we're on land, this mission is mine."

"But this mission involves my submarine, mister, and getting those missile warheads safely on board this boat directly affects the safety of my crew. So, some of my people go along, like it or not."

"I want to send out a recon patrol right away, before the shore party."

"A wise move, I'll let you handle that. If you'd like any of my men to..."

"No, no, Sir. My men can handle that. That's what they're trained for."

"Can I say something?" Rourke asked.

"Certainly, Doctor Rourke," Gundersen nodded.

Rourke saw Natalia, me, even Cole staring at him. "That recon party could be a mistake. We can recon as we go. We have to go from here anyway, regardless of what's out there, only way to reach Filmore Air Force Base. Sending out a patrol from here will only serve to alert any potentially hostile force to our intentions of going inland. I say we move out under cover of darkness, get ourselves well inland before dawn and go from there."

"Bullshit, Rourke!"

"There's a lady present, mister," Gundersen snapped. "And I agree with Doctor Rourke."

"The land portion of the mission is mine. I intend to send a recon patrol out now, I've got men geared up and ready."

Rourke shrugged.

I cleared my throat and pushed my glasses up off the bridge of my nose. "John's right, we let anybody out there know what we're up to, all they're going to do is set a trap for us."

Cole interrupted, "If this meeting is about over, Commander, I've got a final briefing for my men."

Rourke lit one of his cigars, looking at Cole, studying him. "You leading it, the recon patrol, I mean?"

"Corporal Henderson."

"Oh, well, I don't care much if he ever comes back anyway. How's his face doing?" Henderson was the man Rourke had put away for shooting Natalia.

Cole glared at Rourke, saying, "One of these days, Doctor Rourke after we contact Colonel Teal, after we secure those warheads, it's you and me."

Rourke nodded. "It scares me just to think about it," and he exhaled the gray smoke from his lungs.

CHAPTER SIXTEEN

Rourke, Cole, Gundersen, Lieutenant O'Neal and I stood in the sail, watching the dark shore. There was no moonlight, the sky overcast still and the incredibly large flakes of snow still falling, but the temperature still almost warm.

Rourke glanced at the luminous black face of the Rolex on his left wrist, cupping his right hand over it to make the darkness deep enough that the numerals would glow. "The landing party has been gone for eight hours, supposed to be back two hours ago. If they were my men, Captain Cole, I think I might go looking for them."

"Yeah, well..."

"Yeah, well," Rourke mimicked. He shifted his shoulder under the bomber jacket; the Detonics pistols there in the double Alessi rig. The Sparks Six Pack rode his trouser belt, the magazines freshly loaded and each hand cycled through his pistols to assure the magazines functioned properly. These six magazines plus the magazines he normally carried, vastly increased his ready firepower.

Standing next to John, I pulled the Browning High Power, hand cycled the slide, chambering a round off the top of the magazine; then made the 9mm pistol disappear under my Army field jacket.

"Ready when you are, John." I smiled.

"Captain..." It was Lieutenant O'Neal, the missile officer. "Sir, I can get together part of that shore party right now..."

Rourke interrupted him. "Belay that, that's what you say in the Navy, isn't it?"

O'Neal's normally red cheeks flushed as he laughed. "That's right, Sir."

"I've got a better idea, I think, if Commander Gundersen approves," Rourke added. "Cole, Paul, myself, those three other troopers of Captain Cole's, we go in now on a rubber boat if you got one, then get up into those rocks. If that recon patrol Henderson led got nailed, it was probably pretty soon after they hit shore. You save that shore party if we're not back by dawn, and have 'em ready in case we come back sooner with somebody chasing us."

"That sounds good to me," Gundersen nodded. "Captain Cole?" Gundersen raised his eyebrows, as if waiting for Cole to respond.

"No other choice, I guess," Cole nodded.

"I'll get the rest of the gear," I said starting toward the hatchway leading down from the sail.

"And with your permission, Sir," O'Neal volunteered to Gundersen, "I'll get that inflatable geared up."

Gundersen nodded.

*****

The shore was a darker gray line against the near blackness of the water, and in the distance above the rocks which marked the coast, was a lighter gray—it was the sky. The water in the inlet was calm, the deck on the sail almost motionless under him.

I had felt there were people in the darkness, and I didn't doubt at least some of them were watching us from the rocks. As always, despite the elements, the forces of nature, the true danger, was man.

The waves made a soft, almost rhythmical slapping sound against the gunwales of the gray inflatable boat. Rourke crouched in the prow, the CAR-15 ready. I was next to him with my Schmeisser.

Cole and his three troopers filled out the center and aft section, two of the three troopers rowing.

There has always been considerable talk about a sixth sense, but nothing concretely proven, at least as far as I knew. But if there were a sixth sense, and gut feelings... I had one right now.

I shivered, but it wasn't from the cold.

There was a whitish outline gleaming ahead, the shoreline where the waves lapped against it now. The tide was high, and this cut the distance to the rocks beyond the beach.

"Kill those oars," Rourke commanded, stripping away his leather gloves, stuffing them into one of the bomber jacket's outside patch pockets, then dipping his hands into the water on both sides of the prow. "Use your hands," he rasped.

We were barely able to fight the waves rolling back from the shore, to move with the tide and reach the land. Rourke threw a line out and eased into the water, water splashing up over the collar of his combat boot.

Now, I was in the water also. The surf splashed against the prow of the boat, turning into a fine, icy spray. My fingers were cold against the fabric of the boat as we hauled at it, snow still coming down, no more heavily than before, but no less heavily either.

"Come on, Paul," John rasped, then to Cole, "Get your butts outta the boat and give us a hand. Come on!"

Cole sprang from the boat, dousing himself in the water, his three men following suit but with less lack of grace. Water dripping from him, Cole reemerged, cursing.

"Shut up, Damnit!" Rourke snapped. Rourke glancing at me saying, "Together," then we hauled at the rubber boat, over the last roll of breakers, both of us heaving the boat onto the sand.

"You and you, you help 'em," Rourke rasped to the three soldiers. "Get the boat out of here, back in those rocks. Secure it in case the tide does get higher."

Rourke swung the CAR-I5 off his shoulder where it had hung muzzle down. He shifted the rifle forward, working the bolt and chambering the top cartridge out of the freshly loaded thirty-round stick.

We started forward across the sand; we were being watched, waiting for it to come...

It came.

"Kill them!"

The shout was oddly not quite human. Rourke wheeled, snapping the CAR-15's muzzle forward, ramming the flash deflector into the face of the man coming for him. The attacker dropped a machete.

"No guns unless we have to," Rourke half shouted, flicking the safety on for the CAR-15. He stepped toward the attacker, the man starting to move, a revolver rising in his right hand.

I looked up in shock... more of the attackers were coming for me. I heard still others coming toward me over the sound of the waves, over the whistling of the wind. *No guns unless we have to,* I thought. *Well, we have to* and I dumped a Schmeisser mag into faces of those coming for me and started a tactical reload. I saw Rourke's right foot snake out, crossbody, catching a man's gun hand wrist, the revolver sailing off into the darkness.

I jerked the Browning High Power and snap shot two rounds into a bald headed monster. Momentum carried his dead body into me, slamming me sideways into wet boulders.

Stunned by the impact of my head against the rocks, I laid there under the dead man for what felt like a long time unable to do anything but watch. Dazed, I saw Rourke struggling with a man wearing a motley collection of clothing and animal skins. Rourke hammered down with his black chrome Sting 1A knife, the blade biting into flesh somewhere over the right kidney.

My daze lifted and I pushed the body of the bald headed monster to one side and slid out from under him. Two more men, dressed half in the clothes of "civilized" men and half in animal skins, walked slowly toward me.

Unshaven, hair wildly blowing in the wind, one had a long bladed knife lashed to a pole, a primitive pike or spear. The second, bigger but younger than the first, had a pistol in his right hand and a leering, broken toothed grin on his lips.

I shot him first. The first double tap hit him in the chest; he staggered then continued walking toward me. I popped him two more times.

Again, he staggered but did not stop. Every breath pushed a mist of red bubbles from his nostrils and mouth. Four 115 grain hollow points and there were less than ten feet before he would have me.

Pop! Pop!

Another double tap, this time to the face. One passed through the man's open lips and tore out the back of his neck just below the bulge of the brain case. The second slammed into his forehead, a half inch above the bridge of his nose.

Pieces of skull bone erupted and combined with a bloody mist to paint a weird halo around the man's head before he dropped... finally down for good. I spun toward the one with the spear, I squeezed once. The 9mm struck him in the face tearing through flesh but it wasn't a kill shot. The High Power locked open on the empty magazine.

The man's head exploded; Rourke had put two 5.56 tumblers in it. I waved a quick "Thanks," and put a fresh mag in the High Power. I pulled my Schmeisser from under the monster that had fallen on me; wiping gore and sand off of it. I kept hearing, "Kill them! Kill the heathens!" All of a sudden, I was picked bodily up off the beach.

I was locked in combat with a man almost twice my size. My pistol was high in the air, over my head; the wild man fighting me holding it there. I slammed my knee into his groin with all of my power. I thought I broke my right knee...

The wildman doubled over and I shoved the Browning High Power forward as he started to rise, both hands clasped to his crotch. It is funny what you remember... The high pitched pop of the 9mm was almost lost in the wind and the noise of the surf and then, was drowned in the scream of the wildman as he spun out, both hands going to his neck.

He fell.

"Come on, Paul!" Rourke shouted and started toward Cole and his men, the four battling twice that many of the wildmen. I grabbed the Schmeisser as Rourke slipped the CAR-15 forward and telescoped the stock.

I stopped and drew a bead on the wildman, trying for a clean shot and found one. I saw another wildman rushing Rourke from the left. I shouted "Trigger control, trigger control" and sent a three-round burst from the Schmeisser.

The first round hit the man's sternum, the second hit him in the throat and the last punched a hole through the brain case.

I charged forward to Rourke's side as he pivoted toward another wildman with a spear rushing him. Rourke swatted the spear away, taking a long stride out with his right leg, dipping low, snapping the butt of the rifle up in an arc, impacting against the left cheekbone of the man with the spear. His body fell back as I stepped in from the far right, the pistol grip of the Schmeisser connecting against the man's left temple.

Rourke and I were fighting for our lives.

By the time we got to Cole, he was the only one still fighting. A wildman, roughly his own size, blond shoulder length hair falling across his face and half obscuring the irregular beard, was barehanded and had Cole. Cole's rifle was gone and he drew the .45 he'd threatened Rourke with now.

The man he fought swatted it away, the pistol discharging skyward. Cole slumped back, making to fire the .45 again as the blond haired wildman came at him. Nothing happened.

Rourke pumped the Detonics' trigger once; the wildman's head exploding on the left side, the body sprawling back across the sand. For a moment the threat was gone. Cole was looking up at Rourke, then down to his gun. Rourke took four steps forward and reached down, carefully taking the pistol. The slide was only part way into battery, the full metal case 230-grain hardball round somehow jammed diagonally, the bullet pointing upward.

"Odd," Rourke almost whispered. "Jam like that in a military gun. It wouldn't have happened though if you'd fed that round into the chamber off the top of the magazine." Rourke thumbed the magazine catch release, pulling the magazine out, the half chambered round jamming it.

He flashed what I'm sure he hoped was his biggest smile as he gave Cole the empty pistol, the magazine and the loose round and I heard Rourke as he muttered, "Shit" under his breath.

CHAPTER SEVENTEEN

The wildmen chanted, men and women, dressed in the same curious mixture of tattered conventional clothing, animal skins and rags. The shore party Cole had risked was screaming.

Men hanging on crudely made crosses of limbs and scrap lumber were being tortured in a variety of ways. Pyres were set about the bases of each cross and Rourke and I watched now; one of the wildmen reached a faggot into the bonfire which crackled loudly in the wind in the center of the ring of crosses, the ring of crucified men and their torturers.

The faggot glowed and sparked in the wind, it was now a torch.

"Holy shit," I murmured.

"You might say that," Rourke observed.

"What are we gonna do?" It was Cole's voice, his whisper like a blade being drawn across a rough stone.

"That's an odd question for you to ask me," Rourke noted, not looking at Cole, watching the progress instead of the wildman who held the torch. "Now even if Lieutenant O'Neal had his shore party in the boats, should still be ten minutes before they'd even hit the beach. Then another fifteen minutes to climb up here. I'd say that leaves only the three of us."

"The three of us against them," Cole snarled. "You're crazy; there must be a hundred of 'em with guns and more of those damn knives."

Rourke turned and looked at Cole, then at me. "I guess that only leaves two of us. You guard the rear, Cole, your rear. Looks like you're pretty damned experienced at it anyway."

Rourke and I finished moving across the rocks, then slipped down onto the grassy expanse below, hiding in the shadow there while we watched the man with the torch stop in front of one of the crosses.

"Ohh, boy," Rourke whispered.

CHAPTER EIGHTEEN

We both discounted any help from Cole completely. I saw Rourke start forward, searching his pockets for the Zippo lighter, finding it, lighting the chewed stump of dark tobacco in the left comer of his mouth. Again I regretted quitting smoke.

We had reloaded all of our spent and partially spent magazines. If it took us one shot per man and woman around the crosses and they all stood perfectly still while we shot so there would be no chance of a miss, we'd have plenty of ammo to spare.

Right, I thought. *Neither of us had any rounds to spare.*

The CAR-15 was slung crossbody under Rourke's right arm. He stopped walking, less than twenty-five yards from the nearest cross, the one on which Henderson was hung, the one before which the wildman stood holding the torch.

Rourke balanced the rifle butt against his right hip, pulling the trigger once, firing into the air. The chanting stopped, the screaming didn't. The faces of the wildmen and their women turned toward him.

His voice a little above a whisper, Rourke rasped, "You can stop all this or you're dead. Your play, guys."

CHAPTER NINETEEN

"Kill the heathen!"

The man with the torch shouted it, Rourke already lowering the muzzle of the CAR-15, his trigger finger moving once, gut shooting the man where he stood.

The chanting was louder now, drowning out the screams of the crucifixion victims, but not the cries from the wildmen and their women, "Kill the heathen!"

I dropped several men and women on the far side of the ring of crosses. I kept my focus spread between available targets on my side and covering John.

A wedge in the wildmen opened and I could see the wildman John had gut shot had somehow crawled toward the pyre beneath the cross on which Henderson was hung, and the pyre was beginning to burn.

Rourke started to run toward the cross, the flames licking higher, fanning, it seemed, by their own heat, higher pitched than the screams and curses and threats of the wildmen, the scream from Henderson. "Help me!"

It surpassed pandemonium; it was chaos on steroids and LSD.

As I fired, I could hear Henderson's screams. They were beyond what could have come from a human. I glanced and saw flames licking at the skin of his bare legs, his screams unintelligible save for the agony they expressed.

I was clear for the moment, but two men were charging Rourke. I ran to him. Rourke pumped the trigger, the Detonics bucked in his hand once, then once again. I dropped on one knee and braced my High Power in a firm grip and squeezed. The first shot spun the man and the second dropped him.

A man Rourke had shot was getting to his feet, a torch in his hand. The man swung the torch, Rourke stumbling back, firing the Detonics and hitting the wildman executioner in the face twice, the head exploding like an overripe melon hitting concrete. I had found a jeep and was streaking to John's side from the far side of the ring of crosses.

On the ground near the base of the cross was a machete. Rourke grabbed it and looked for a way to reach past the tongues of flame. The flames were too high, too hot. I heard Henderson still screaming and saw John fall back. "Look out, John!" I yelled as loudly as I could.

Rourke wheeled, the Detonics in his left fist punching forward, fired out. Rourke holstered the Detonics and shouted, "Paul, drive her into the base of the cross and jump clear, hurry!"

The empty CAR-I5 hung by its sling as Rourke drew the Python from the flap holster at his hip, double actioning one of the 155-grain jacketed soft points, point blank into the chest of one of the wildmen.

One of the wildmen was clambering onto my hood. Rourke pushed his right fist to full extension, double actioning another round from the six-inch, Metalifed Python, missing and then firing again. The second shot caught the wildman on the hood of the jeep in the left side, the body rolling off, gone. Rourke jumped back, my jeep crashing through the flames at the base of the cross.

I jumped clear, rolling, coming up, my subgun firing into the wildmen.

Rourke snatched up a fallen machete from the ground, shifting the Python to his left fist, jumping the flames at the perimeter of the pyre and reaching the cross. Henderson was screaming, his legs afire.

Rourke dropped the revolver and the machete, lowering his hands into the damp ground and the light covering of snow. Scooping up handfuls, putting them on the flames, he started for the ropes on Henderson's left wrist, recoiling for an instant; spikes had been driven through the palms of the hands.

Rourke started to work at the massive nail driven through Henderson's left palm; he stopped. He raised the man's left eyelid; Henderson had died.

From then on, John and I simply fired, stabbed and killed. It was a slaughter.

CHAPTER TWENTY

John and I stood back to back, fighting the circle as it was called. It was the only way to cover each other. "Gotta move on those crosses," Rourke shouted.

"Of the ones I've freed," I shouted over the steady roar of the Schmeisser, "only two of them are able to move; one guy on the ground is using an assault rifle I liberated."

"Let's get outta here, free the rest of the men to carry the ones who can't walk, fight our way back toward the beach," Rourke said and started moving.

"I'm almost outta ammo," I told John.

He shouted back, "Let's run for it, beat ya to the nearest cross," then started out at a dead run, keeping low, the CAR-15 spitting fire. The nearest cross had a man clinging to it who seemed half dead, blood dripping down his wrists and forearms but no spikes driven through the palms of his hands.

"Lemme," I shouted, shifting the German MP-40 back on its sling, putting an open pocket knife between my teeth, then jumping for the cross's spar, reaching it, wrapping my blue jeaned legs around the stem and the man on it, then freeing one hand, sawing at the ropes.

Rourke had his black chrome Sting lA out, hacking with it now at the ropes binding the ankles to the cross's stem.

"One hand to go," I shouted.

The man called down from the cross, "God bless you both!"

John held the man by the legs as I tried guiding him down. The man's sweating, shivering body was covered with clotted blood from lash marks across his chest and back, stab wounds in his thighs and upper arms.

"Could you handle a gun, even from the ground?"

"Yeah, a gun, yeah," the man mumbled. Rourke nodded, rising to his full height, picking a target with an assault rifle. He started toward the wildman at a loping run, firing the CAR-15 as the man turned around.

Rourke was beside the body the next moment, wrestling an M-16 from the dead man's grasp, searching the body, finding what he sought. Three spare twenty-round magazines.

Rourke grabbed up a M-1 carbine from another dead man, searched the body under the rags and animal skins, found two thirty-round magazines in a jungle clip and was up and running.

From more than two yards away, Rourke hurtled the M-16 through the air. "Paul!"

I caught it, wheeling, stuffing my High Power into my trouser band, the M-16 spitting fire into three men running toward the cross, handguns blazing.

Rourke dropped to his knees again beside the injured man. "Here, use this," and Rourke gave him the M-1 carbine and the spare, clipped together magazines. "We'll be back for you," Rourke shouted.

As we raced toward the last cross, firing the CAR-15 into the wildmen, I could see that more were coming. I started to climb the cross and shouted, "This one's dead."

"Paul, get the men you released earlier, if any of them are left, meet me at the far side."

"Right!" I said jumping to the ground and running. The next time I caught sight of John he had a Detonics in his left hand and a riot shotgun in his right.

Rourke flipped the shotgun in his hands, starting a baseball bat swing, hitting a man with a spear full in the face with the butt of the riot shotgun. He dropped the scatter gun and ran the ten yards or so to the injured man with the M-1 carbine who fought from his knees at the base of the cross from which he had been hung.

John leaned close to the dying man's lips and listened, then frowned... then the man died. Rourke shouted to me, "Let's get outta here, up into the rocks." We had two survivors. "You get the other guy out," Rourke shouted, running back to the second trooper. "I'll get this one."

When we reached the base of the rocks with the two surviving members of the advance team, there were still the rocks to be climbed.

*****

My Reflection:

Writing these words can no more convey what was happening than reading them will. Throughout history, men have tried to explain combat, describe it... dissect it. It can't be done.

Someone said once that unless you have been in it you can't understand it and for those that have been in it... there is no reason to try and explain it. We kept killing... killing until the people we were killing ceased to be human beings. And for a while I fear... we did too.

CHAPTER TWENTY-ONE

"Paul, we can't haul these guys any further!"

"I know," my voice came back, sounding odd.

"If I don't get out and you do..."

"I'll get back and I'll find your family, I swear it to God, John."

"And Natalia..."

"I'll take care of her..." I had already made up my mind to save a round... I could not let John be taken alive. Death by a friend was better than death on those damnable crosses; far better.

We held the pistols ready. The isolated shouts and curses were gone, but the voices now becoming one voice, a chant, the words chilling my soul.

"Kill the heathens! Kill the heathens! Kill the heathens! Kill..."

Rourke turned to look at me; I held the pistol, the battered Browning High Power, clutched in my right fist. My left hand, as if an automatic response, moved to the bridge of my nose, to push back the wire framed glasses.

I held my fire, waiting on John to decide they were close enough.

*****

My Reflection:

Since the time I met John Thomas Rourke... there were many times I thought I was going to die. But there were actually only a few times when I felt real fear in those moments. It was almost always like I was detached from myself... like I was watching a movie or TV show.

John had always said, "It's okay to be scared, it's okay to get the shakes. It's okay to cry and it's okay to throw up... but try to do it after the crisis has passed. Do it in those quiet moments afterwards when the thoughts and memories come rushing in on it. Stay in the moment, it will save your life and if saving your life means a bad guy has to die..."

My issue became I feared I was losing my humanity with all of this killing and death. I mentioned that to John one time, he shrugged and said simply, "A man that loses his humanity probably can find it again. A man that loses his life..." I saw his point.

CHAPTER TWENTY-TWO

What the hell is he waiting on? I wondered. *I can see the whites of their eyes in the torchlight glare reflected from their steel.*

He opened fire and then I did, my pistol barking beside him. *Trigger control, trigger control,* I kept thinking.

I heard the twin stainless Detonics pistols belch fire again and again and saw bodies tumbling, spinning out, falling... My High Power belched and more bodies spun and tumbled, but more bodies swelled the ranks behind them; a wave, a human wave that seemed endless.

I felt rather than heard John's Detonics go silent and then my gun fell silent. Then there was a shot burst, then another... *the wildmen, they were using their guns?*

Another shot burst, M-16 fire as best I could tell and bodies going down from the leading ranks of the wildmen storming toward us.

"Rourke! Doctor Rourke!" I heard the shout but didn't look to find the source. Rourke fired, I fired, the men in the rocks fired. The wildmen died... a slaughter.

"Rourke!" a voice cried out, Commander Gundersen, running, a .45 in his right fist, two seamen flanking him, firing M-16s.

Gundersen was beside us. "I've only got fifteen men, all I could spare from the ship; we gotta get the hell outta here."

"Wait a minute," Rourke rasped. He walked forward, finding what he sought. He wrestled an M-16 from the hands of a dead wildman and found a half dozen magazines and a second M-16.

"We gotta get outta here, Rourke!"

Rourke nodded, handing me an M-16, distributing the magazines evenly between us; it was still a long way to the beach.

CHAPTER TWENTY-THREE

Natalia told me later she had been shivering in the conning sail of the submarine when she heard gunfire from rocks above the darkened beach. "Sailor," she asked, "what did Commander Gundersen instruct you to do if the shore party couldn't get back?"

"He told the Exec to pull out, Ma'am, least that's what I hear, Ma'am."

"What if the shore party is coming back, but under fire?"

"We're to guard the deck, Ma'am, that's it."

"Not return fire to cover them?"

"Against orders, Ma'am," and he smiled.

CHAPTER TWENTY-FOUR

One of Gundersen's landing party was dead, the body being carried slung in a fireman's carry by one of the other sailors, still another wounded in the left arm, but firing an M-16 with his right.

Gundersen said, "I'm already getting my men down with those two crucified men, got three more helping them, then to get the inflatable ready and into the surf."

"They're gonna pick us off as we climb down the rocks on the far side," Rourke told Gundersen matter-of-factly. "Unless we break up; Paul can take three men and so can I, fire and maneuver elements to cover the rest of you getting down."

CHAPTER TWENTY-FIVE

I took my three men and laid down cover fire for John and his three as they advanced. They ran quickly to a set of boulders and set up to return the favor. I along with my three got ready to make a run for it.

I rammed a fresh stick into my liberated M-16, the rifle coming up to my shoulder, one of my three man squad to my left, the other two behind and slightly above me. Gunfire was starting again. I squeezed the trigger of the M-16, letting it go forward almost instantly. A perfect three-round burst. I made another, then another, bodies.

Trigger control, trigger control. I found myself laughing as I fired. *Insanity*? I had no time to consider that, I realized.

"Trigger control!" I shouted at the man next to me who had let off seven shots in a burst. As I fired again, I laughed again, murmuring it to myself as well. "Trigger control, trigger control, trigger."

My fire team was under heavy assault rifle fire from the rocks above, on the last leg of the fight toward the beach, a fight it appeared we might lose. I was counting on John's team to provide enough firepower to hold the wildmen back until we reached the surf, but unless a fire team remained behind to cover the withdrawal, it would be hopeless. The boats would be shot out of the water.

My three men hit the beach. I was still in the rocks, firing. Rourke had ordered his own men to set up a firebase to cover loading the boats and then he ran back into the rocks where I was pinned down.

"Paul!" Rourke screamed my name. "Paul!"

"Go back, John, I'm outta ammo!"

I had my rifle inverted, the butt stock forward, swinging it, two more of the wildmen coming for me. I swatted one of the men away and started running, then Rourke fired at the other. The man fell back.

One of the boats was already away. I heard Rourke's voice over the din of the battle. "Paul! Hurry it up!"

"I'm trying, Damnit!" I shouted as another of the wildmen came up on me, less than ten yards away with an assault rifle. Rourke fired, the man going down.

"Get his gun! Get his gun, Paul!"

Rourke covered me as I stretched for the M-16 and two magazines. Then I jumped from the nearest rock, now less than three yards from Rourke.

The dark silhouette of the submarine was visible, perhaps two hundred yards from shore. Perhaps O'Neal would get to the decks in time, or Gundersen. At the distance, accuracy would be nil, but heavy concentrations of fire aimed high enough to provide against bullet drop, might work.

CHAPTER TWENTY-SIX

There were only two boats left when the deck gun opened up and figures in the rocks fell. John pointed at me and the six men with us. "Let's catch those last two, come on."

Rourke splashed into the surf where the one man who'd remained with the boats hunkered down, his M-16 ready, the salt spray and foam washing over him.

The six sailors and I were running into the surf, our legs freezing as the water soaked through our pants and boots.

Suddenly, waves flooded over my boat. We were thrown free as the boat upended. I had time to shout, "John!" but only once and then things went dark.

I can barely remember feeling a tug... Rourke had found me in the water and grabbed my shoulder rig. Rourke was dragging me up, shouting "Paul! Paul!"

Swallowing ocean water, I gagged out, "I'm all aww, shit, all right," coughed and doubled up with a spasm. Blood pumped from my head; there was gunfire all around me.

CHAPTER TWENTY-SEVEN

Though I don't remember it, we made it back to the submarine. Later, I found out that Gundersen couldn't decide whether to court martial who ever gave the order to open fire on the beach or give him a medal.

When he found out it was Natalia, he settled for buying her a drink.

She had slugged a young sailor and taken his M-16. She fired a burst into the air and told the sailors on the deck, "Those men in the boats, the ones still on the beach, they'll never make it if we don't do something. We can fire into the rocks; fire high so we won't hit our own men, lay down heavy fire. Three-round bursts, keep it pouring in there, please!"

"Orders Ma'am," one voice called up to her. "We ain't s'posed to fire."

"Sailor," she almost whispered. "I'll kill the first man who doesn't; those are your comrades out there, only you can save them."

Natalia Anastasia Tiemerovna had shouldered the M-16 again, her abdomen hurting badly from the unaccustomed exertion.

"Yes Ma'am," and then the sailor turned to the rest, "You heard the lady, if we're gonna disobey orders, may's well do a fucking good job of it!"

Afterward, the crew secured the sub and Gundersen ordered the boat to dive.

CHAPTER TWENTY-EIGHT

The "drink" had devolved to a glass of orange juice; Natalia sitting in her borrowed bathrobe beside Rourke in the officers' mess.

Doctor Milton determined that when a wildman with a machete overturned the rubber boat, I got hit with the butt on the machete in the head while I was grappling with him. Milton said I'd be okay, just sore for a while.

Gundersen was not happy. "We're going to have to find another area to try another penetration. The boat's ammo stores are seriously depleted, and more importantly the manpower. We lost six dead, have fourteen wounded in all."

Cole, who just happened to appear just as our last rubber boat was about to take off, interjected, "We've still gotta get to those warheads, the hell with those wildmen or whatever they are."

The bottom line was there would have to be another attempt to contact Colonel Armand Teal and take control of the nuclear warheads. It would have to be a small, well-armed force to penetrate the airbase.

CHAPTER TWENTY-NINE

By the time I was back on my feet, Rourke and the ship's armorer had broken down and cleaned our weapons. Salt can do terrible things to a fine gun and it doesn't take long.

Rourke told me Gundersen had stopped by to discuss the operation to Filmore. He said that Natalia wanted to go along, and he was letting her go. Rourke had argued, "She's too weak, and it's dangerous anyway..."

Gundersen countered, "Cole wants to kill you as soon as you get to the missiles, maybe before then. And he will have three of his own men on the trip."

Rourke nodded, he told Gundersen that one of Cole's men he had tried to rescue from the cross had told him that Cole isn't who he says he is, whatever the hell that meant. Rourke said he wanted Lieutenant O'Neal and me on the mission.

CHAPTER THIRTY

The submarine was already pulling out to deeper water, and then would dive to resurface near the original site of the battle with the wildmen. To draw them off, they hoped.

Cole asked, "You ready, Doctor Rourke?"

"Yeah."

Natalia, her eyes so incredibly blue, her skin more pale than it was always. She looked at John and so did I, we both felt the tension with Cole.

"I make it due north a ways," Cole called out.

Rourke looked at Cole, then started to walk, Natalia and I flanking him. Her pack was light, but I knew that soon John or I would wind up carrying it.

"Due north?" Cole called again.

Rourke kept walking, through his teeth, the word barely audible, "Yeah."

CHAPTER THIRTY-ONE

She was tired. "Paul, you asked to take my pack... take my pack, please," she said. I turned toward her. She stopped walking, swaying a little.

Rourke asked her, "Are you all right?"

"Of course she isn't all right; taking a damn Commie woman with us was fuckin' stupid, Rourke!" Cole said.

I watched Rourke, he closed his eyes. He opened them; he bit down hard on the stump of cigar in the left corner of his mouth.

"Cole, I make it we've got a day's march left to Filmore Air Force Base and Armand Teal, but I just can't take another day of your mouth."

Cole didn't move. "Yeah, well, too fuckin' bad, Rourke."

"Thought you'd say something like that," Rourke said.

"You lookin' for a fight, Rourke?" Cole shouted, laughing.

"Yeah."

"Well," Cole smiled. "Well, you gonna take off your coat and your guns?"

"I won't need my guns, and no sense taking off my jacket for something that won't take much time."

"Now look, Rourke, we got a job to..."

"Shut up," Rourke said.

"The hell," Cole moved, his right fist drawing back. Rourke sidestepped, turning half away from Cole, Cole's left hammering forward, Rourke's left foot snapping out, a double kick into Cole's midsection and chest.

Cole stumbled back, Rourke bringing his left foot down, wheeling, his right foot snapping out, catching Cole in the chest and the left side of the face. Cole went down.

Lieutenant O'Neal tried to stifle a laugh. He wasn't doing a good job of it.

CHAPTER THIRTY-TWO

Cole stayed quiet and to himself. Rourke watched him as they walked because he distrusted him. But at least the fight had silenced him.

Natalia moved well, but without the usual spring to her step. I still carried her pack, Rourke having taken her rifle. The woman now walked only with the double flap holsters containing the custom Smith L-Frames President Sam Chambers had given her.

Rourke stopped in the fading reddish sun, I could hear him say, "O'Neal, without having your people change their pace, without anything, tell them to be ready for it, we've got company."

O'Neal started to look up.

"Don't, up in those rocks to our left, gonna spring it on us when we reach the end of the defile, maybe just before."

Rourke quickened his pace, but only slightly, leaving O'Neal gradually more and more to his rear. Nearing Natalia and me, he said, "Here, Natalia, carry your rifle, gonna need it. Up in the rocks I saw something catch the sun. Rifle maybe, I figure they're up there."

Cole and one of his troopers led the ragged column. Rourke, slowly, caught up with him. "Cole, up in the rocks. We've got company. Don't act differently, just keep walking."

"Aww, shit, if we hadn't brought the woman we woulda been outta here by now."

"Shut up and listen. These guys weren't following us, probably got Filmore Air Force base ringed, but that's a good sign. Must mean somebody's alive in there. We just cut in on the wildmen, they weren't following us."

"I feel like I'm playin' Cowboys and Indians."

"Yeah, well, good similarity, I guess. When the shooting starts, you and your private there take up positions on each side of the defile and start pumping up into the rocks. I'll take the others through, then Rubenstein and I will set up covering fire from the other side of the defile for you and your man to get through, then we try for Filmore as fast as we can."

"What're ya gonna do about the woman?"

"Carry her if I have to, she's my responsibility. You just do what you've gotta do and it'll work out." Rourke slowed his pace, risking a glance up into the rocks, he saw movement, but indefinite movement, he wasn't certain.

He looked ahead as he slowed enough for Natalia and me to catch up with him. The defile narrowed into a wide "V" shape as we reached the height of the rise.

Natalia said, "I feel them, up there, waiting."

"Yeah, me too," I said.

"When it comes… Paul, you get Natalia through," John said.

"I can take care of myself." Of course, I knew she would say that.

"Paul," John said, "you do what I say, then set up on the other side of the defile. As soon as I get through with O'Neal and his men; Natalia, you stick with O'Neal. Paul and I'll be covering."

A gunshot, a heavy caliber, echoed across the defile. A scream. O'Neal shouting, "They got one of my men!"

Rourke shouted, "Run for it!" firing up into the rocks.

"Come on, Natalia!" I shouted and we ran for the defile's V-notch. Cole and his private were already in the notch, firing up into the rocks. O'Neal's men ran toward the notch as well. Automatic weapons fire came down from the rocks.

Natalia and I made the V-notch; bullets impacted and ricocheted off rock faces on both sides of us. Rock chips pelted us, the dust from the rocks thick as automatic weapons fire hammering the rock walls.

I positioned Natalia next to me with the Schmeisser and I opened up with the M-16 behind a heavy piece of granite boulder. I pushed up and sent two three-round bursts into the rocks. Gunfire hammered into the boulder.

Cole and his private hunkered down in the V-notch, firing up into the rocks. Rourke ran past them, throwing himself through the gap and rolling. The rocks on both sides seemed to explode with ricochets and dust.

Rourke saw us and pushed to his feet, half ran, half threw himself toward the protection of three massive boulders. "O'Neal, take Natalia with you. Paul and I will cover you from here."

"Here we come," Cole shouted.

A moment later I shouted, "They're through, come on, John."

"Get going," Rourke shouted. I was up and firing a burst half over my shoulder into the rocks.

Rourke and I ran, turning every few steps to pump shots up into the rocks. Beyond the V-notch there had been a rocky trail, narrow.

The ricocheting sounds of bullets hitting granite stopped. Ahead of us was a valley. Natalia sat on her haunches; I stooped over beside her, her face pale, her head between her knees. O'Neal's left arm was streaming blood, but he stood erect. One of O'Neal's men lay on the ground, the front of his pea coat stained and wet with blood.

Ahead, I could see the outline of a fenced military enclosure, Filmore Air Force Base. There were small craters in the far side of the valley, to the north. Nothing grew in the valley, brown trees, brown grass; I couldn't hear a bird chirp.

"What the hell happened?" I asked.

Rourke looked at me. "Neutron bombs, the craters are from the impact areas."

"John," Natalia, pale, closing her eyes as she spoke, turning her face up toward the sky, her voice odd sounding. "Why did they stop shooting, why are they not following?"

"Everything that was here is dead, they're afraid of radiation. Natalia, when you can, take care of O'Neal's bleeding."

He stood and to the rest said, "We can rest here for a little while, move out into the valley in a few hours, Paul and I'll take the Geiger counters and run point for radiation."

He looked at me and said, "Paul, get my medical kit, got a bullet to take out here."

*****

My Reflection:

Why did some of humanity sink back into barbarism and some not? Why did some people allow their hate, their brutal nature to take over?

Why did some people show the very best of human kindness and decency while others showed the very worse? Maybe someday someone will be able to answer these questions.

I certainly can't.

PART TWO
MEETING THE PROPHET

CHAPTER THIRTY-THREE

The climb down from the rocks to the base had been hard for Natalia and hard for the wounded as well. Rourke carried Natalia's M-16, I had her pack. Cole and his two men had hung back, a rear guard against a further attack by the wildmen. I doubted they would come into the valley until they realized we had not died from radiation.

Out in front of the rest, I walked; the wand of the Geiger counter extended ahead, occasionally sounding the all clear. John had told me, "If you find a hot spot, by the time you got the reading on the Geiger counter, it will be too late to save yourself. We don't have any decontamination equipment."

Rourke walked with Natalia beside him. I heard John shout to Lieutenant O'Neal and the rest, "Veer off toward that small canyon over on the left, we can rest there."

Then he called out to me. "Paul, pull back and head toward that small canyon, get some rest!"

"Gotchya." When I got there, Rourke and Natalia were discussing getting to Filmore Air Force Base and Cole.

*****

A few hours' rest had turned into an exhausting night for all. But Rourke was anxious to reach the base, find the six eighty-megaton warheads housed on the experimental missiles, return to the submarine and get Commander Gundersen to take us back.

We had lost now two weeks in the search for Sarah and the children.

.We could see the main entrance to Filmore Air Force Base. The fences appeared wholly intact and the base itself seemed untouched. There were bomb craters in the far distance beyond the base. John said the base likely had been hit early, not with bombs, but ICBMs with neutron warheads. No plane would have gotten this far in the early hours of the Night of The War.

That the field itself was untouched was just luck, missile guidance systems weren't precise enough to drop just outside the base's perimeter and leave the base untouched, ready for us again.

"John," Natalia said.

"Yeah, I saw it." Rourke looked at her for an instant, then back toward the base itself, a reflection from a water tower not far inside the base fence line. Glass perhaps, glass from a scope.

"When I give the word, fan out, fast," he said loud enough that Cole and his troopers and I would hear. I nodded, and glanced toward the field. I had seen the reflection as well.

A sniper would have predetermined fields of fire and ranges. There would be range markers.

I heard Natalia rasp, "There is a small pile of rocks by the side of the road twenty yards ahead, the rocks are darker than most of the others here."

"Take cover!" Rourke shouted and pushed Natalia with his right hand, running left.

There was a loud crack. Rourke shouted, "Throw some fire up toward the water tower!"

Natalia, Cole, and the two U.S. II troopers carried M-16s; my German MP-40 a close-range weapon was useless at this range.

Rourke threw himself to the dirt, the CAR-15 snapping up to his right shoulder, his legs spread wide. He jumped up and started to run again; the heavy caliber rifle from the water tower firing again.

We kept running, the fence now twenty-five yards.

"Gotta go over the fence!" Rourke shouted.

"Electrified!" Cole shouted now.

"Bullshit, not enough power, I hope!" He kept running, five yards remaining. "Cole, you and your men, keep that sniper tucked down. Paul and Natalia and I'll go over first."

"Barbed wire, John!" I shouted. Rourke didn't answer. His left hand was reaching out for the fence as he threw himself against it, his right boot finding a brace against the chain link. He snapped the rifle up, the butt plate caught the top line of barbed wire and Rourke hauled himself up, freeing the rifle.

The sharp crack of the sniper's rifle, a loud pinging sound as he glanced right, the nearest vertical support for the chain link was dimpled and bright. Rourke slipped out of the bomber jacket, throwing it over the barbs. "Paul!"

I ran toward the fence. Rourke throwing his weight down and to the side, further compressing the barbed wire. I went past him, up, over, and dropped. "Natalia!"

It was her turn. She went past him, up, over the fence. She landed as gracefully as a cat after the twelve foot drop. She was already moving, her M-16 spitting fire. I was running also, with a slight limp.

"Cole!" The fence shook and rattled again, then Cole was up, past him, dropping, the man after him stopping at the top of the fence, firing a burst from his M-16. Natalia and Cole were laying down assault rifle fire inside the compound now.

I opened up with the Schmeisser; it was perfect for close up fighting.

The second of the U .S. II troopers went up and over the top of the fence. Rourke hauled himself up, leaving the CAR-15, its sling entangled in the broken section of chain link, leaving his bomber jacket as well.

He hauled himself to the top, throwing his weight over, sideways. He dropped, hitting the dirt hard, losing his balance, rolling.

He pushed himself up, snatching at the Detonics .45 under his left armpit and then the one under his right. He started to run. The heavy-caliber rifle discharged again, into the concrete near his feet as he once more hit the road.

Natalia and I were next to a sentry house fifteen yards to Rourke's right and he aimed for it. I was now firing up into the water tower with my battered Browning High Power from about seventy-five yards at least, all but useless. Natalia pumping neat, three-round bursts from her M-16.

72

Rourke reached the sentry house, slamming against it, catching his breath; Natalia firing again. He looked at her, leaning down as he did, putting his head toward his knees.

"Are you all right, your... your ear..."

Rourke touched his ear; blood came back on his fingers. Frowning, he said, "Are you all right, how's your abdomen after going over that fence?"

"I can tell where your suture line from the operation was," she smiled. "But I'm all right, you're a good surgeon. Let me look at your ear."

"No time, gotta..."

"Let me look at your ear," she ordered, stepping closer to him.

"Paul!" I turned toward them, Rourke looking up, Natalia handing me her rifle. "Try this."

"Right," I nodded, pushing my wire-rimmed glasses back off the bridge of my nose. Then I took the assault rifle and leaned around the edge of the sentry house. The sniper rifle fired again, the report louder this time.

"".375 H&H maybe," she said absently.

Rourke nodded, sucking in his breath hard as she touched at his ear. "Paul, you were limping."

"I'm fine, just gave myself a little twist, worked it out when I ran."

"Good." Rourke nodded, gritting his teeth. I could tell he was fighting the pain again, as he felt her probe the wound.

"It's bled enough, I don't think there's risk of infection; medical kit is in your pack?"

He nodded.

"I think the bleeding is stopping."

"Cole?"

"Here!" The U.S. II Captain's voice came from behind a truck, a two-and-one-half ton, parked just beyond the second gate, the gate swung closed now but nothing locking it as Rourke glanced down the road. "There's maybe three or four guys in that low building!"

"Keep 'em pinned down, assume they've got a lot of ammo, so don't worry about burning up yours," Rourke called back.

He looked at me. "Give Natalia back the M-16, we both head through the gates, then you to the left and me to the right. Once you're inside twenty-five yards of the tower, find some cover and keep burning sticks into the tower. I'm climbing it."

"Let me, you'll start bleedin' again." I said.

"No," and Rourke turned toward Natalia. "You keep him pinned down, the sniper, keep him pinned down while Paul and I make the run, then give Paul some fire support while I climb. We'll be okay, that scope won't help him at the distance."

"All right," she nodded, her blue eyes wide. "Be careful."

"I always am," he whispered. The Detonics stainless .45s in his fists, he glanced at me. "You ready?"

"Aww, sure," I smiled. "Nothin' like a good running gun battle to start the day off right."

"Let's go," he rasped through his teeth. He hit the gate a half step ahead of me, shoving against it, the gate swinging wide. I was keeping up with him, I pushed my glasses up on my nose again as I ran. I was nearing a Jeep.

"Go for it, Paul; watch out if he hits the gas tank!"

"Gotchya!"

We kept running, there was the rattle of subgun fire then the huff and puff of Rourke catching his breath and I watched him working his way around to the rear of the water tower.

Assault rifle fire hammering into the timbers from the low blockhouse ebbed. Rourke safed both Detonics pistols, holstering them in the double Alessi rig and started up, hand over hand, diagonally, following the pattern of the cross timbers.

More assault rifle fire hammered into the timbers around him, then Cole and his men, Natalia and I fired. Between magazine changes, I watched him keep going, judging the distance remaining as perhaps thirty feet. I sent a burst from the Schmeisser and there was a boom from the sniper rifle.

Twenty feet to go. Rourke reached out for a timber above him that gave way. Losing his balance, Rourke reached out with his hands, finding the diagonal reaching support, his feet swinging in midair, and then he found purchase. He started up again.

Fifteen feet to go.

Rourke kept moving, more assault rifle fire coming at him, more answering fire, then the original fire ebbing. Ten feet. Five feet.

John stopped and I watched him look up, then lower the muzzle of his Python. Assuming that the sniper must have him covered, I was swinging my weapon on line when I heard someone shouting, "Hold your fire! These are friends."

CHAPTER THIRTY-FOUR

The fire from the blockhouse stopped. The sun was fully up on the horizon now. It was quiet except for the shuffling of feet on the road surface below as the blockhouse began to empty.

*****

We followed Armand Teal to his office. Teal handed John the rifle he had used against us. It was a .375 H&H Magnum. "Bought the rifle, had it custom stocked and the barrel bedded. The thing would print minute of angle at two hundred yards with an el cheapo scope on it. Figured the rifle was fine but needed a better scope. My son was in Germany, he picked up the Kahles for me when he was on a leave." Teal stopped talking.

Rourke cleared his throat, finding one of his dark tobacco cigars, lighting it in the blue-yellow flame of his Zippo. "I, ahh, I understand a lot of our people survived over there, still fighting the Russians, maybe Fletch is still alive."

"Yeah," Teal nodded, licking his lips, looking away. "Yeah, maybe, maybe he is."

Rourke exhaled the smoke.

Teal searched for words, "See, ahh, we don't know much here. Like you said about this new thing, U.S.II and Sam Chambers being President. Last I knew he was filling a new Cabinet post, science and technology."

"He was the only one left."

"How is he, I mean... a good President?"

"He's got problems, he's trying his best," Rourke told him honestly.

"You sure we can trust her?" Teal asked, looking at Natalia sitting between them, then at Rourke.

Natalia spoke, "I am Russian, I don't want your people to have any more weapons. But I don't want either side to use any more. I'm his friend. You can trust me until I tell you that you can't," she answered for Rourke.

"Seems fair," Teal shrugged. "Anyway, nothin' top secret about it. See, the Night of The War, like you folks call it, well. Ever heard of EMP?"

Rourke nodded.

"ENP?" I asked.

"EMP," Teal corrected.

"Electro Magnetic Pulse," Rourke added.

Natalia said, "A detonation sends shock waves through the atmosphere, the bigger the detonation and the higher up it is, the greater the shock wave effect, roughly."

"Mustn't have been too big or you folks woulda known about it," Teal said, his eyes moving, shifting from us toward the other side of the conference table, where Cole sat.

"Wiped out all our communications, destroyed the printed circuitry in all our aircraft. Nothing got off the ground after the first scramble. I don't even wanna think about those guys up there, suddenly, all their electrical systems go out, no communications, they..."

Teal fell silent for a moment. "We got the communications restored after a while, scrounged up all the old vacuum tubes I could find and we made up a working radio. Couldn't reach too far with it though. Got several of the helicopters and a dozen fighters to where they'd work. Figured we'd at least have something our guys could use when we got help. But, ahh..."

Teal lit a cigarette. "Got plenty of these, the BX just sent a shipment in a day before it happened. Enough for a couple thousand guys hooked like me for quite a while, you know?"

"How did you survive, Colonel?" Cole asked.

"With everybody on alert, I ahh, I was in the command bunker here. With the intelligence people, you know?" He puffed on the cigarette. "In the intelligence vault. We got hit, no warning at all. The Security Police Senior

Airman on vault duty jumped for the door and slammed it shut, he was on the outside.

"I wrote up a commendation for him; don't know if he has a family left to know about it. He saved our lives, though. For what, I..." Teal looked at his cigarette. "I thought, when we tried our communications, when we didn't get anybody. I thought maybe we were the last ones. All the old frequencies, dead. Lot of Soviet jamming. Didn't know, only eighteen of us survived the whole thing, most electronic intelligence guys, couple of senior officers.

"There were television security monitors inside, that was before the pulse. We watched the missiles falling, thought we were all right, but then people just started dying. You could watch 'em just dying. Sick, just, ahh..."

Teal stopped, stubbing out his cigarette and lighting another. Teal sank his face into his hands. I thought I heard a sob, covered up with a cough, and then Teal looked up, his eyes wet.

"Thought maybe, well, we were the only Americans left at all, anywhere."

"Couldn't bury the guys when we got out," Teal continued. "Just too many of them, thirty-four hundred and twenty-eight, not just guys, women, too. Some wives and kids, my wife... you remember Martha, John, right?" Rourke nodded.

Teal stood up, his chair falling backward, slamming and echoing against the concrete floor. He walked away from the table, Rourke watching him, knowing everyone else was watching him, too.

There was nothing to say...

CHAPTER THIRTY-FIVE

We sat outside the bunker, the sun strong at nearly midday. Rourke was eating a Milky Way from the BX, Natalia smoking from a fresh carton of cigarettes. "This is my favorite brand. I always liked your American cigarettes," she said suddenly.

"We hauled all the bodies," Teal began again. "Hauled em, over there" and I followed with my eyes where Teal gestured, a burnt-out hangar across the field. "Took us, well, a long time. And the bodies, well... by that time. We couldn't use a wooden structure, afraid the fire would spread. Had plenty of aircraft fuel though. So we doused all the bodies with it.

"One of the Airmen, from Kentucky I think... Well, he worked at a fireworks factory for a while. Said he knew how to blow things up. We let him do it after I... I prayed."

Rourke asked, "What about your position here, I didn't see eighteen men. The wildmen? That why the sniper post?"

"Yeah, that and the Russians if we ever see 'em, guess we aren't important. Wildmen, good a name as any," Teal laughed. "See, I'm the only qualified pilot. And I couldn't leave the base, give up my command, maybe there would be something we could do, you know? So I sent out four men, just to get the lay of the land. They had decontamination, everything. Should have come back. But they never came back, not at all."

Teal lit a cigarette. "See, we didn't have any idea about the outside world, figured the only way I could tell what to do, if there were anything to do, anything... I decided to risk three more men, if I could get volunteers. Well..."

Teal threw down the cigarette, stubbing it out under the heel of his combat boot.

"I got 'em," he sighed. "Only one of 'em returned. But he died right away afterward. He talked about these crazy guys, half civilized, almost half animal, like somethin' out of some el cheapo sci-fi movie, ya know?" Rourke nodded.

"Anyway, they killed their victims by burning 'em on crosses."

"How did this man escape?" Natalia asked, putting out her cigarette against the concrete steps on which she sat, her M-16 across her knees.

"Cut to pieces with some kind of spear, least that's what he said it was. He was a tough guy, had the survival training course. Found a stray wildman, killed him with a rock. Took some of his clothes, used the guy's spear like a cane or a staff, he hobbled in, almost dead already."

Teal paused, lighting another cigarette, "Fletch's age, John, just a kid. Died in my arms. That gave me eleven men," Teal said, his voice low. "I wasn't gonna risk anybody else. Figured to wait and see. That was three weeks ago.

"One of the guys, an officer, shot himself in the mouth with a 45. Another, Airman Cummins, got what we all figured was appendicitis. Boy, we could have used you, John. We don't have a doctor. I tried, got the medical books out, tried. He died."

"If it ruptures and you don't know what to do, the poison spreads pretty quick," Rourke said soberly.

Teal continued, "Yeah, it was kinda quick. So I got nine men and myself. I got five sleeping right now, one man guarding 'em. Three others, sentry posts around the base with the best excuses for sniper rifles we could come up with. Lotta guys had personal weapons we had logged in and locked up.

"Picked the best we could find outta those. These aren't so good for long distance stuff," and he tapped the butt stock of the M-16 on Natalia's lap. "We held the base though," Teal concluded, then fell silent.

"The wildmen," Natalia said, half to herself. "They must think there is still radiation here. That must be why they haven't attacked."

"But with us coming in, they'll probably figure it's safe," I said.

Cole spoke then. "I came for the missiles you store here, and wildmen crazies or not, I've gotta have 'em, Colonel. I've gotta..."

80

I studied Cole. When he said, "I've gotta have 'em," I thought he had finally spoken the truth.

CHAPTER THIRTY-SIX

Rourke sat in the cockpit of the prototyped FB-IIIHX, running the preflight check, Armand Teal on the access ladder beside him, coaching him. I was plugged into the intercom the flight chief normally used, listening. Rourke had told Teal he had never flown an F-111-type aircraft.

"That's your targeting computer there." Teal gestured, pointing past Rourke.

Rourke nodded. "Where are those missiles Cole wants?"

"About seventy-five miles away from here, past the wildmen, as you call 'em," Teal's voice echoed across the otherwise still hangar. "You're never gonna get 'em out with those crazies out there.

"Reconnaissance should tell the story, John. From what I figure and what you and the Russian woman told me, well. Those crazies are all over. We're trapped here unless we get out by air, and I can't leave this base intact. Goes against everything I was taught, everything I believe. Leave it to fall into enemy hands. Never. The President could even order something like that, and I wouldn't. Only way to get those missile warheads out is by air. And that means chopper 'em here at least and then put 'em on a B-52."

"The Soviets could pick off a B-52 using their radar," Rourke said.

"Then you'll still need to use helicopters to get them out to the submarine. The Russian woman flies?"

"Yeah." Rourke nodded, looking at him.

"Well, there's your answer."

"I haven't seen a helicopter anywhere on this base."

"Three of 'em in the last hangar on the end. Army choppers, Kiowas. Had 'em flown in here just before the Night of The War. There was a joint services exercise being planned, never got all the details."

"That hangar locked?" Rourke asked him.

"You're thinkin' of Cole, right? I don't trust him either. And, yeah, it's locked." Teal saluted and stepped down and back from the plane.

Rourke looked back to the instrument panels, hit the switch and I could hear the whine of the engine starting to fill the plane.

CHAPTER THIRTY-SEVEN

I felt almost civilized again, riding in a truck cab with someone else doing the driving. It was a definite improvement over walking out to get Lieutenant O'Neal and the others from the shore party.

There were two trucks; I looked back in the side view mirror through the dust cloud, and an ambulance was following behind. My driver was Airman Standish; he was black, and the man who had worked at the fireworks factory in Kentucky, the man who had taken on the grim task of setting fire to the corpses from the Night of The War.

"What are you folk doing here?"

I said, "Looking for six missiles."

"The experimental ones?"

"Yeah."

"They're a long way from here, fella." Standish laughed, gesturing up toward the high rocks beyond the boundary of the valley. I saw what he pointed at, wildmen.

CHAPTER THIRTY-EIGHT

We returned to the base with O'Neal and his people. I rested for an hour and then decided to try and fix the radio.

I adjusted the power wattage selector, then checked the modulation indicator; an Airman Stephensen was sitting beside me. "You know," the airman laughed, "for a couple amateurs, we're doin' okay with this old radio."

"The U.S. II frequency for contact is easy to find, but they'll have to contact us after they pick up our signal, if they pick up our signal," I told him, trying to fine tune the squelch control.

"Where'd you learn about radios?" Airman Stephensen asked.

"I was gut shot a while back. In the infirmary where I was, there were lots of military manuals, I started reading up on radios, only thing I had to do. Then I took it easy for a while at John's Retreat, read about radios there too and lots of other stuff."

I stood up from the antiquated radio set, pushing the metal folding chair back and walking across the room in the lower level of the bunker, stretching; my back hurt.

"What's this Retreat thing you keep mentioning?" Stephensen asked as he turned his chair around and lit a cigarette.

"The Retreat," I shrugged. "Well, John planned ahead for a war, or whatever. He was a survivalist for a long time. I guess he was a sharper reader of the times than most people, I don't know. But he's got this place in the mountains, in Georgia. Worked on it for years, comfortable, all the conveniences, must've cost him a fortune."

"Before The War, was he a doctor, like a surgeon or something?"

"No," I said smiling. "No, he studied but never practiced medicine. After the CIA, he got into teaching survival training, about weapons, writing books about it, I guess some of the books sold really well. He was in demand all the time. Spent every free dime he could get on the Retreat. He told me once he was always hoping his wife would be able to say, 'I told you so,' and the Retreat wouldn't prove out to be anything except an awful expensive weekend place. Told me it was the only time in his life, the only thing he did in his life that he wanted to be proved wrong about. Guess he wasn't," I added, thinking it sounded lame.

"Yeah, well, I figure the world's gonna end."

"Yeah? Why?"

"Well," and Stephensen raised his eyebrows, his voice dropping a little. "Well, God said in the Bible he'd end the earth again, but by fire, you know? And nuclear weapons, they're fire. Probably all of us'll get radiation sickness. If there's any babies born, probably be deformed and all, ya know? I think it's God punishing us for gettin' too smart, maybe. Too smart for our own good, like Adam and Eve did; you got Adam and Eve, don't ya?"

I nodded. "Yes, Adam and Eve. Jews have Adam and Eve, too and Noah like you were talking about with God's promise after the flood. We've got 'em."

"Then you know what I mean." Stephensen nodded, looking up at me.

"Yeah, I know what you mean." I nodded, going back to the radio set. "Let's see if this sucker works."

I sighed, hearing the door opening behind me. Turning to see who entered, I saw Cole holding his .45 automatic and his two men M-16s. I stared at the muzzle of the gun, my right hand by the radio, not near enough to my body to reach the butt of the High Power in the tanker holster across my chest.

I started to speak, my right hand very slowly moving across the receiver to the frequency dial. I would need to feel three clicks right on the dial to be on Rourke's frequency. By moving my left elbow I could jam the push-to-talk button down at the base of the microphone.

I did that, saying, "What do you want, Captain?"

"It's what I don't want, Mr. Rubenstein. Are you and this guy contacting U.S. II headquarters?"

I dialed and felt one click. "Why not?"

"Might be embarrassing, they won't understand."

Two clicks, one more remaining until I reached the frequency for Rourke's fighter bomber.

"Where the hell is Colonel Teal?"

"We were waiting for them. Got 'em all."

I wanted to push up, out of the chair, but I kept my left elbow against the push-to-talk button at the base of the microphone. I felt the third click.

"Where's Armand Teal, you kill him, too, Captain Cole?" I made the question to instantly brief Rourke, if he was listening. I didn't want to hear the answer myself; I knew it would be a death sentence.

CHAPTER THIRTY-NINE

"Teal's got a bump on the head and his hands tied. We lined up everybody else and shot 'em. And with Teal as a hostage, once Rourke and that Russian bitch land, they won't be able to go after us in a plane, couldn't risk killing Teal. I got the ball and I'm keepin' it now."

I said, "I don't think John will let you get your grubby hands on those missiles."

"Doesn't bother me if he tries to stop me. Once I get to them, they don't go anywhere but up, all away." Cole turned slightly, BLAM!

"You just... you just shot Airman Stephensen in cold blood, damn you!"

Cole's voice then, "Cold blood, hot blood... what the fuck's the difference."

BLAM!

CHAPTER FORTY

I was back in the surf, drowning. I could not tell which way was up or down. I could not move; the only good thing I realized was I did not hurt. *No pain,* I thought, *there is some gain.*

I saw people in the distance walking toward me. Walking on the sea bottom, then I saw her... Ruth, Ruth Bixon, my fiancée. My beautiful fiancée. But that couldn't be.

She waved and ran to me calling my name, "Paul. Paul, oh Paul." She looked so sad. "Paul, Paul." She kept saying.

"Ruth, I'm right here," I said.

"Paul, Paul... Oh, Paul, wake up!"

I did.

It wasn't Ruth, it was Natalia and she was holding my head with both hands. She said, "There is so much blood." She smudged at it, watching as my eyelids fluttered.

"Paul, Paul. Wake up."

At that exact moment I could suddenly tell up from down and I hurt. I hurt like hell and I moaned.

"Easy Paul, take it easy. I have you."

I smiled and whispered, "John... tell John Cole is bad... Tell..."

"John knows Paul, he heard the transmission. Can you sit up? Can you stand?"

"Don't know. Head hurts." The room swam in circles and suddenly I was back under water.

*****

"Paul, stay awake, you have to help me. You have to stay on your feet. I'm not strong enough yet to carry you." Natalia coaxed me.

I know that, I thought. *I'll stay on my feet.*

"Okay, now sit down, slowly."

Stand up, sit down. Damnit Natalia, make up my mind what I am supposed to do. No, sitting down is good. I'll just sit here.

Suddenly I was back under water.

CHAPTER FORTY-ONE

Rourke was kneeling next to the bodies and must have heard the noise of the Jeep behind him. He reached for the Detonics and spun to face not a threat but Natalia driving the Jeep and me sitting next to her rubbing my head.

Natalia had brought me back to life, a minor miracle. But Cole was no less culpable and Cole was going to die.

Natalia cut into a slight curve to her right, the Jeep skidding on the concrete hangar flooring with a squeal of brakes. She jumped from the driver's seat, as John stepped up into the Jeep to inspect my wound.

Gingerly pulling back the bandage Natalia had improvised, John said, "You have a hard head, Paul."

"Shit, I... I feel like somebody, somebody hit me with a sledgehammer."

Rourke laughed, still inspecting the wound. "Over two hundred thirty-grains of jacketed lead traveling slow and steady isn't anything you should expect to feel good about."

Rourke shaking his head, looked at me. "I heard your transmission and after I landed, we found these bodies in a hanger. Cole and his bunch killed everybody on the base, except O'Neal and hopefully Teal. O'Neal is wounded ..." he turned back to the man, trying again to save O'Neal's life.

Groggily I asked, "So I guess he either got Colonel Teal to tell him where the missiles were or figured he could sweat it out of him."

"Why the hell would somebody make missiles with such big warheads?" I asked.

"Should I tell him?" Natalia asked, not smiling at all. Rourke only nodded and continued to work on O'Neal.

"Paul," she began, patient sounding, as though explaining to a child. "Once the idea was the larger the warhead, the greater and more formidable a weapon. Then your country began searching for greater accuracy in delivery systems, like the MX missile. A smaller warhead that could reach to a target with virtual pinpoint accuracy has greater destructive capability on hard targets than something huge and dirty. These were soft target warheads. A soft target is a population center. A hard target is a missile silo, a command bunker, something made to withstand everything except a virtual direct hit."

It suddenly hit me. "And if Captain Cole is so knowledgeable as to be able to take control of these missiles and their eight megaton warheads..."

"Then we must assume," Rourke interrupted, "that he knows how to fire them and already has targets in mind." Off in the distance I heard a muffled gun shot.

For quite some time he worked on O'Neal. Rourke said, "O'Neal will live, the wound to his neck is deep and bloody but packed now and the bleeding stopped. But he is very weak." Rourke studied the man's face, O'Neal still not conscious, but sleeping rather than in a coma.

"Why are we sitting here, then?" I asked.

"Cole won't kill Teal until he knows where the warheads are," Rourke said. "We have to wait. Before I made the flight, Teal told me there were helicopters here, in a locked hangar."

Natalia came back, jogging quickly. "The hangar you sent me to was locked and shuttered. I shot the lock off and found helicopters, OH-58A Kiowas. The choppers have been repaired, three machines, but only two of them would start."

Rourke frowned, "So, after Cole gets what he wants out of Teal, he'll keep Teal alive just in case Teal deceived him or a special access code is needed as insurance against Natalia and me and now you."

"He must have transportation, probably another Jeep. He has to cover seventy-five miles cross country, with time out to work over Armand Teal, while watching out for the wildmen to attack. I figure sometime tonight he should be there. We go airborne after dark and look for signs of Cole and the others, then we do whatever the situation allows. Or..."

"Or demands," Natalia interrupted.

"When we were airborne," Rourke said, "we saw signs of wildmen massing for an attack here." Rourke glanced at the black faced Rolex on his wrist. "Probably in an hour, maybe an hour and a half."

"Natalia, I want you to preflight two of those helicopters. Paul, you stay here with Lieutenant O'Neal. I've done all I can for him and I think he'll survive. I'm taking the three-seater fighter up. I'll strafe the wildmen just to let them know we're interested and kill as many of them as I can since they'll be so conveniently assembled. I'll land the thing somewhere nearby with a nearly full fuel load.

"You and O'Neal will be on your own for a little. Natalia will fly me back here, we'll take both helicopters and search for Cole and the others. Natalia will show you what to do after she preflights the choppers.

"You and O'Neal, he should be awake enough to keep an eye on your back, can sabotage all the remaining aircraft on the field here.

"This base is a loss; when Natalia and I get back, we'll rig the ammo dump and the arsenal to blow..."

"But couldn't we use that stuff ourselves?"

"Yes, and we'll take what we can. Get it all aboard the craft and still leave room enough for our bikes if we can get 'em back off the submarine."

CHAPTER FORTY-TWO

Rourke and Natalia returned and picked me and O'Neal up in the choppers. Neither of us were a hundred percent but we were better. We beat Cole to the bunker that held the missiles.

"There would have been a crew here, wouldn't there?" Natalia almost whispered.

Rourke didn't look at her, peering into the darkness as he walked. "No, these missiles were off line as far as I could tell, which is why they're still here and not in a billion pieces somewhere inside the Soviet Union. Cover the right."

"Yes," we heard her answer.

He smiled at her, and then turned away, walking slowly, steadily, toward the bunker. I was behind him with the Schmeisser and O'Neal, carrying his .45 Government Model, was bringing up the rear.

Rourke stopped at the steel door of the bunker. Natalia's voice: "There should be a conventional locking arrangement, then a second door inside with a double combination lock."

"Can you work the combinations; I did poorly at that in spy school."

She laughed. "I was very good at it; a woman has a naturally more sensitive touch. I can, but it would take perhaps a few hours without mechanical assistance, I don't think the stethoscope from your medical kit would help a great deal with the types of doors they have."

"You're well-informed," Rourke told her.

"Yes," she called back.

He turned shouting, "Paul, if these locks will keep us out, they'll keep anyone else out except Cole or Teal. You and Lieutenant O'Neal, I want you..."

"John!" Natalia screamed and we all wheeled. From the top of the bunker where it was partially mounded over with earth, one of the wildmen was lunging for Rourke with a double-headed axe, the handle cut to hand-axe size.

Rourke took a half-step back. Hearing the shots from Natalia's M-16, the wildman spun out in midair, crashing down. Something hammered at John from behind. He stumbled forward under its weight, the Car-15 falling from his shoulder. A Bowie pattern knife, long-bladed, cheap looking but deadly enough, stabbing, biting into the ground beside his face.

I moved but couldn't get a clear shot. Rourke jabbed his right elbow, the arm already extended back, the elbow connecting with something solid, the wildman crumbling off Rourke's back. John rolled, snatching the Detonics .45 from under his left armpit, jacking back the hammer, firing at the face three feet away from his hand.

The wildman's head exploded, blood spattering upward. Rourke pushed himself back, pumping the trigger of the Detonics .45 at the same time as bursts from Natalia's M-16 and my Schmeisser. The battle was over quickly but not quickly enough. Luckily we were all still standing.

Well, actually I was leaning against the wall... utterly exhausted.

CHAPTER FORTY-THREE

Lieutenant O'Neal, originally a missile officer from the sub, told Rourke, "Disabling these missiles will be very tricky, impossible once they are armed. This was an irretrievable or No-Recall system. Once they are armed, the only thing you can do is fire them."

Still leaning against the wall of the bunker, I pushed myself away from the doors. "That's stupid!"

"Yeah, a lot of us thought so," O'Neal nodded, shifting his position on the ground, obviously uncomfortable. "Nobody asked us, though. It was supposed to guard against Soviet sabotage of our missile systems."

"Well, then, what'll we do?" I asked

Rourke looked at me. "Natalia and I fly back to the submarine with the two helicopters and bring back reinforcements. Shouldn't be more than two hours, three tops. Those wildmen we killed were foragers, I guess. Either that or something like a patrol. These doors are bombproof, so they weren't trying to get into the bunker, you can see from these scorch marks where somebody tried it, likely some of these guys, and they learned they couldn't."

"If I'm wrong and there's a big concentration of wildmen coming, get out, we'll pick you up. Fire a flare from that H-K flare pistol of mine."

"There are flare guns in the helicopters." Rourke glanced at Natalia.

"Better still. So, either way," Rourke said, taking his rifle from where it leaned against the bunker doors, "it shouldn't be rough duty. Stay up in those rocks. If Cole comes, keep him away from the bunker. The wildmen come, beat it out of here and they'll keep Cole away. Then we can try to do something about getting inside, that may be where you come in," Rourke said, looking at Natalia.

She laughed.

"What's so funny, Major?" O'Neal asked, his face wearing a strange expression.

"A KGB major being aided in breaking into an Air Force missile bunker by the United States Navy."

I said it. "She's right, that's funny."

CHAPTER FORTY-FOUR

"Mr. Rubenstein! Wake up!"

I opened my eyes, feeling warm, sleepy still from my painkiller induced sleep, and then I moved. I shook my still throbbing head, snatching up the Schmeisser, then getting to my knees. Across the small depression where the mounded over bunker was on the far ridge, I could see wildmen massing. And now, faintly, I could hear the rumbling of vehicles. I saw the first one, a battered Jeep rolling up on my far left on the ridge. Then, on my right, another Jeep.

And then at the center, a massive pickup truck, the wheels high off the ground and suspended from the winch supports at the front of the vehicle was a body. Burned black in spots, blood covered, the left arm missing, the eyes catching the glint of sunlight and reflecting it like glass, it was Armand Teal.

"Look!"

"I see him," I murmured to O'Neal.

"No. No, look!"

I turned toward O'Neal, then past him. Wildmen. Wildmen on either side, heavily armed with assault rifles, spears and machetes, some of the wildmen standing like toy figurines, almost frozen, their spears poised for flight. And at their head. "Cole, you son of a bitch!" I shouted, horrified.

"Mr. Rubenstein, you and Lieutenant O'Neal, lay down your arms!" Cole shouted.

"Bullshit!"

"Lay down your arms and you'll be spared, at least for now. I came for the missiles, not to kill you!"

I worked back the bolt of the Schmeisser, pushing O'Neal aside, on my knees still, the submachine gun snaking forward. I fired, Cole dodged but two of the wildmen with him went down.

A shadowy thing that flew was in my line of vision, tearing into me, dragging me back and off my knees. I felt myself spread eagling, the subgun still firing, upward, my left arm not moving. I looked at the arm; a massive stick seemed to be holding me to the ground.

O'Neal cried, "A spear... my God, Mr. Rubenstein!"

"Spear..." I coughed the word, my subgun fired out. I tried to move my left arm, felt the tearing, the ripping at my flesh. "No!" I screamed the word.

CHAPTER FORTY-FIVE

A lot of what happened next remains in a blur from coming in and out of consciousness. Off in the distance somewhere, I felt more than heard a sound, a beating sound. I realized that I had been tied to the cross. Groggily I looked around. O'Neal was struggling against the rope that held him to his cross.

Wildmen were everywhere, and in the middle of them stood our two crosses. Near the crosses, I could see Cole and his two men, Armitage and Kelsoe. Beside them sat a bizarre, squat looking man wrapped in a bearskin robe.

Cole was pointing at the sky; I looked up... two helicopters. John and Natalia and with them men from the submarine flying low, giving as little advance warning of their arrival as possible.

Then... then they banked sharply and flew off toward the other side of a ridge. O'Neal screamed, "Come back! For God's sake come back. Don't leave us." I watched until the two choppers disappeared then I guess I passed out.

*****

I hung helpless on the cross, in and out of consciousness for I don't know how long. O'Neal wasn't moving and I didn't know if he was still alive or not. Then he turned his head toward me, fear and pain etched on his face.

I couldn't move but I could see and off in the distance I saw him walk down from the top of a rise, passing a half dozen wildmen that did not see him. It was John Rourke. Then I passed out again.

I felt a hand on my ankle, checking for my pulse, John. Then heard someone say, "Give me your guns."

It was a wildman, large, armed with an AK-47. He had reached out his left hand. Rourke, the cigar in the left corner of his mouth, reached up his left hand and took the cigar. He stared at the wildman's hand for a moment, cleared his throat and spit, the glob of spittle hitting the wildman's palm.

CHAPTER FORTY-SIX

"You son of a bitch," the man snarled, Rourke sidestepping half-left and wheeling, his left foot snapping up, feigning a kick at the head. The wildman dodged to his left leaning forward.

Rourke wheeled right, both fists knotted on the CAR-15, his right fist pumping forward with the butt of the rifle, the rifle butt snapping into the wildman's chest. Rourke tore the flash-deflectored muzzle down diagonally left to right across the man's nose, breaking it at the bridge and stepped back, just short of killing him. His right foot stomped on the barrel of the AK-47 as the huge wildman tumbled forward and sprawled across the ground.

The wildmen were starting to move, Rourke's rifle's muzzle on line with Cole. "Call 'em off, asshole!"

"They'll rip you apart," Cole shouted back.

"Let's see what the man wants first, shall we?" Rourke shifted his eyes left, to the squat man in the bearskin.

"Cut 'em both down, now!" Rourke snarled.

Cole smiled, "No."

Rourke's eyes met his eyes. "You're a dead man already, on borrowed time."

"Cut them down," the squat man in the bearskin commanded. Rourke stepped back, his eyes flickering from Cole to the wildmen starting toward the two crosses.

A burly, tall man started up the cross where I hung, hacking at the ropes, Rourke snarling to him, "Let him down easy or you get a gut full of this" and he gestured with the CAR-15.

The man climbing the cross looked at him, nodding almost imperceptibly. Others of the wildmen started forward, catching me as the ropes were released, helping me down, setting me on the ground. Rourke shot a glance to me. Through a haze and fog I could make out his face. Through my parched lips I said weakly, "John?"

"Yeah, Paul," Rourke almost whispered. "It's okay. Take it easy," Rourke told me, watching Cole then and shifting his eyes to O'Neal as they brought him down from the cross.

"I'm dyin' on my feet, damnit!" I said through clenched teeth.

Rourke looked at me and edged forward gesturing the wildmen away with the muzzle of the CAR-15. "Get ready," he said and reached down, pulling my right arm across his shoulders, getting me up and slumping against his left side. "All right?"

"Yeah," I sighed.

Rourke said nothing, looking at O'Neal, lying there. O'Neal seemed somehow more subdued, more ill than when he had been on the cross.

"Okay, Paul, we start forward, right?"

"Right," I nodded, my breath coming in short gasps, but regular. Rourke started to walk, half dragging me on his left side, the CAR-15's muzzle leveled now toward Cole and the squat man in the bearskin and Levis.

He kept the muzzle in the airspace between them, he whispered, "If either one moves, I'll shoot the man in the bearskin first." The wildmen, a knot of them closed around us as we moved forward.

"You'll never get outta here alive, you Jew lovin'..."

"Shove it, Cole," Rourke snarled. Then he stopped, less than two yards of air space separating us from Cole and the man in the bearskin.

"I'm called Otis," the man in the bearskin smiled.

"No shit," Rourke nodded.

"You are, ah?"

"He's John Rourke, Dr. Rourke," Cole said through his teeth.

"Ohh, the John Rourke who wrote those excellent texts on wilderness survival, how marvelous to meet you after reading your work, I literally devoured them. And the books on weapons as well."

"Marvelous," Rourke told him.

"Since I know so much about you, I suppose... well, that you'd like to know something about me and about my little band of followers here."

Rourke said nothing.

"He's loony, John," I coughed. Rourke still said nothing.

"We actually call ourselves the Brotherhood of The Pure Fire. I'm the high priest, the spiritual leader, the mentor to these lost souls, one might say."

"One might," Rourke whispered.

CHAPTER FORTY-SEVEN

The squat man grinned, "Yes, well, as you can imagine, after all this war business, well, the time was ripe for someone..."

"To appoint himself leader of the crazies," Rourke interrupted.

Otis, the wildman leader smiled. "In a manner of speaking, I suppose so. But of course our mutual friend here, I think he makes me seem mild. After all, blowing up Chicago with five eighty-megaton warheads is a bit extreme, isn't it?"

Rourke's eyes shifted to Cole's eyes, Cole's eyes like pinpoints of black light burning into him. "Now's the time you're supposed to say, 'You'll never get away with this,'" and Cole laughed.

"I'm more of a patriot than you, hangin' around with Jews and Commies. I'm gonna rid the United States of the Soviet High Command."

"President Chambers never sent you, neither did Reed."

"Reed? Hell, I almost hadda shoot Reed when I killed the real Cole and took his orders. Nothing but bullshit with Reed and Chambers, they'd never have the nerve to push a button, but me."

Rourke said nothing, then murmured, "Good-bye," then pumped three fast rounds in a burst to Cole's chest. Cole, or whoever he really was, fell back, screaming, his hands flaying out at his sides.

"My missile!" Otis screamed, his voice like a high-pitched feminine shriek, a broad-bladed knife flashing into his right hand from a sheath at his belt. Rourke shifted the muzzle of the CAR-15 left, firing, but Otis dove toward him, the slug impacting against Otis' right shoulder, hammering the man back and down, but not killing him.

As Otis fell back, his body rolled against a mounded tarp behind him, part of the tarp whisking back, Teal's burned and mutilated body, the eyes still open in death, was on the ground, insects crawling across the face. The wildmen were closing in, knives, spears, assault rifles in every hand. Rourke pumped the CAR-15's trigger, unable to miss, firing into a solid wall of humanity.

I lurched away from him, unsnapping and grabbing the Detonics .45 from under John's left armpit in one motion. The heavy bark of the .45 rumbling too now, the gunfire from our rear unmistakably that of an AK-47.

"O'Neal!" Rourke shouted.

Rourke snatching at the Detonics .45 under his right armpit, thumbing back the hammer, firing point blank into the face of the nearest wildman, the body sprawling back, others falling from its weight.

Rourke's right hand flashed to the flap holster on his hip, getting the Python, the six-inch barrel snaking forward. He edged back, firing both handguns now, the Detonics in his left, loaded with seven rounds this time, and the Colt in his right, loaded with six. Both guns were half spent as he edged back from the knot of screaming, howling wildmen. He looked skyward for an instant, the heavy, hollow chopping sound of helicopter rotor blades suddenly loud over the shouts of the men trying to kill us.

"Natalia!" he shouted.

The green OH58C helicopter was coming in low, and now fire was spitting from the side gun, the 7.62mm slugs hammering into the knot of wildmen, their shrieks louder now as they ran for cover.

"John!"

Rourke looked behind him. I was beside a massive pickup truck. Rourke started to run toward me, the Python bucking in Rourke's right fist as he snapped the last three shots over his left shoulder, then threw himself into a run, automatic weapons fire already starting around him, then dove for the shelter of the vehicle.

I was on my knees, pale as death beside the right front wheel well, firing out the Detonics, empty. Rourke slammed closed the cylinder of the Python, the Safariland speed loader, empty now, crammed back into his musette bag. He handed the pistol to me, "Here use this."

Rourke took the Detonics, emptying his own pistol, then reloading both with fresh magazines from the Sparks six pack on his belt. He reached into the musette bag, getting the remaining loaded magazines for the CAR-15, putting them on the ground beside me. "You recovered fast."

"Bullshit, I'm dying, just too stupid to fall down."

"Lemme look at that" and Rourke slipped behind me, probing gently at the wound. Rourke reached behind his back, snatching the AG Russell Sting lA from the sheath at his belt, using the blade to cut away the sleeve.

"Aww, that was my good coat, John."

"Shut up," Rourke snapped. "The wound is dirty, clotted; I'll have to open it to clean it. You think it hurts now, wait'll I get around to fixin' it!"

I pushed my wire-rimmed glasses back up the bridge of my nose. "Coulda been worse, John, coulda lost my glasses."

"Yeah, could've at that," Rourke said, leaning against the pickup truck. "Remember how to hotwire a car?"

"Yeah, I remember."

"Gimme that rifle and climb up there, once you've got it going, I'll pass up the CAR and the spare mags. We'll head for the bunker, make a stand there, and run over as many people as we can on the way, huh?"

I smiled, handed Rourke the rifle and reached up for the door handle. "Shit, it's locked!"

"I'll fix that" Rourke said. "Look away." Rourke reached for the Python at his hip, aimed at the lock and turned his face away, firing upward, the thudding sound loud of lead against sheet metal.

"Now try it."

I pulled at the door handle. "Hot" and the handle broke away, the door swinging out. I grinned, and then started up into the pickup cab, gunfire coming from the sky again as Natalia's helicopter made another pass.

The truck vibrated, coughed, then rumbled, the engine making sputtering sounds as it came to life. Rourke edged up, grabbing the spare magazines, then throwing himself up beside me. "Can you drive this thing one handed?"

"You just shift when I tell ya," I shouted.

"Right," and Rourke, the Python back in his right fist, tugged at the door, closing it partially.

Wildmen running for the truck, Rourke's right hand swinging the Python online one round, a head shot. A man down. Another round, then another, two in the chest and a man down. He fired out the last two; a double shot at a wildman with an M-16, the rifle discharged a long ragged burst spider-webbing in the glass at the top of the windshield.

Rourke and I could see the bunker now through the partially shattered windshield and there was a man near to it, near the doors, the doors opening.

"Cole!"

CHAPTER FORTY-EIGHT

Natalia's chopper banked to port then banked again lining up the greatest concentration of wildmen, around the massive, oversize-wheeled pickup truck then it leveled off. The rattling of the M-60 machine gun mounted in the door could be heard over the rotor noise. The ground was plowed up under the impact of the heavy slugs as the gunner from the submarine walked the rounds in toward the target.

Cole disappeared inside the bunker doors as bullets hammered against the concrete surrounding the doors and into the doors themselves. The chopper pulled up, banking steeply to starboard again, climbing, then nosing down toward the ground. Natalia was going after the wildmen on the ground blocking John and me in the truck.

We would go after Cole.

The bunker was less than a hundred yards away now; Rourke firing at targets of opportunity, occasionally the truck lurched as I would free my right hand to pump the CAR-15 through the driver's side window.

Gunfire from the wildmen and from the submarine's shore party. At the doors of the bunker now Rourke could see a second figure, O'Neal. He stepped back, kicked out, ramming his foot against the outer door of the bunker, then falling onto his knees, firing his pirated AK-47 at the locking mechanism.

Rourke pumped the triggers of the twin stainless Detonics pistols, the truck grinding ahead over the bodies, hurtling bodies to each side. I ducked as gunfire ripped into the windshield again. Rourke fired out both pistols, nailing the wildman with the assault rifle.

Forty yards to go, Rourke one pistol through the open side window, killing a man there, then pushing open the door, standing up, holding to the truck cab, shouting to O'Neal, "Back away, we're gonna ram the door."

"Paul, get into a crouch behind the wheel, I'll jump clear. Leave her in second and give her all the gas you got!"

"Right, gotchya," I shouted back.

Rourke jumped clear when we were about five yards from the door, the roar louder still as I hammered the gas pedal flat against the floor. Then screeching and grinding as the truck slammed into the bunker door. Then all was quiet except for the sound of my racing heart.

John appeared beside the truck shouting, "Paul!"

I looked up. "All right, okay. I'm all right."

"Down!"

Rourke punched the Detonics pistol in his left fist forward. He fired three times, emptying the pistol, mutilating the face of the wildman with the butcher knife starting for me through the sprung open driver's side door.

I rolled against the seat back, pushing up the CAR-15, firing through the open door behind John as more of the wildmen rushed the truck. Rourke threw himself up, over the hood of the truck, swinging his legs over and dropping down, firing the pistol in his right hand at a man with a spear as he hit the ground, then pushing himself through the space between the metal door and the jamb.

Through the crack between the door and the jamb, we could see wildmen massing for an assault against the door, the one called Otis, blood oozing through his fingers as he held his shoulder.

"Paul, you and O'Neal get as far back as you can go, hurry." Rourke edged back, away from the door, the assault starting. As we ran deeper inside, Rourke fired the Detonics, hitting the truck's fuel pump.

The truck roared into an explosion.

Suddenly we all were gasping for air, the heat of the explosion making a wind, sucking air from inside the bunker. There was screaming outside.

Rourke pushed himself to his feet and half threw himself into the deeper shadow ahead, down the tunnel leading into the main body of the bunker. We followed. Cole would be arming the missiles to launch and millions would die.

CHAPTER FORTY-NINE

We came to a second door, the one with the combination lock. It was wide open. "You two stay here. Thank God, had Cole closed this, we would have been powerless to stop him." Having said that, John raced ahead.

We turned and faced back toward the front of the bunker, where the wild-men would come for us. I could hear the humming of machinery, generators working the lighting and the missiles' firing devices were all on the same electrical system, I assumed.

I heard Rourke shout, "Cole, don't!"

Then I heard Cole shout, "For America!" Then there was gunfire, shots ringing out again and again. Suddenly the lighting switched from whitish yellow to a dull red, a mechanical voice booming over a speaker.

The computer voice announced, "T minus ten minutes and counting, irretrievable launch sequence initiated. T minus nine minutes forty-five seconds and counting."

Next to me, O'Neal said, "Shit."

CHAPTER FIFTY

Suddenly, I heard Rourke shouting, "Calling the helicopter! Come in, damnit!" He must have found a functional radio.

Natalia's voice squawked back, "John, where are..."

"No time..., in the bunker, launch is..." The mechanical voice came again, "T minus eight minutes fifty seconds and counting."

"You hear that?"

"Yes, yes!"

"Get down here, I'm going into the silos, try to disarm the electrical system that would trigger the launch. The panel here is armor plated and I can't get into it. Follow me, we've gotta try, Rourke out!"

I heard the clang of his footsteps on the metal steps. As he ran, I prayed.

CHAPTER FIFTY-ONE

Outside I heard the chopper rotor noise and gunfire between the landing party forces and what remained of the wildmen. O'Neal and I moved back to the door of the bunker, the one I had crashed into with the monster truck.

There was more gunfire and I heard Natalia, "Follow me. Follow me to the bunker. I have to get inside! Follow me!" More gunfire.

A second later I heard her holler, "Get that squat man with the bearskin, he must be the leader." More seconds and I heard, "Paul, it is Natalia, I must get inside!"

I looked at my watch, perhaps five minutes remained before the launch. "Paul."

"Come ahead, Natalia!" She ran past us without looking.

CHAPTER FIFTY-TWO

The mechanical voice droned on, "T minus five minutes twenty-five seconds and counting. T minus five minutes twenty seconds and counting. T minus five minutes fifteen seconds and counting."

In the distance I heard Natalia shout, "Shut up" as she ran.

"T minus five minutes five seconds and counting. T minus four minutes fifty seconds and counting. T minus four minutes forty seconds and counting."

This time I hollered, "Shut UP!" I wondered if Natalia would make it in time.

The computer voice droned on. "T minus four minutes twenty seconds and counting." I thought, *Doesn't the voice know that it too would die.*

"T minus four minutes five seconds and counting." The voice was maddening.... "T minus twenty-five seconds. T minus twenty..." The voice was swallowed in the roar of the missile engine.

*****

Rourke and Natalia had failed, now they would die in the flames of the rocket engine and so would O'Neal and I. Time stopped... It was over. John Thomas Rourke was over.

I could hear the rumbling of the engine, the sound was incredible. I knew O'Neal and I must leave the bunker or die by the flames from the launch.

Suddenly, I heard John... "Paul, get outta here, run for it."

"John! Natalia!" I shouted.

"Go, run!" Rourke shouted back.

We ran! We ran like I had never run. The doorway, five yards. Two yards!

Natalia was through, then O'Neal and me. Rourke threw himself through and past the burnt truck.

"Down!" he shouted.

The fireball belched out as we rolled, our hands going up protect our faces. Then it was gone.

I looked up... no missile contrails were in the air. We all lay there, breathing. "How... How did you finally do it?" I asked breathlessly.

It took several minutes for Rourke to answer. "Natalia thought of it. We couldn't stop the countdown for ignition. She removed the insulation around the launch control panel so that when the first missile ignited... its fire would melt the circuits to prevent the launch."

"How did she know it would work?" O'Neal asked.

"I didn't..." Natalia said sitting up, her face red and tender. "Not for sure." She looked at John. "You have the worst sunburn I've ever seen," she laughed.

Rourke put his arms around her and held her body close against him. He closed his eyes.

*****

My Reflection:

When you are in a combat situation, time has a way of changing. Minutes can seem like hours, hours can seem like seconds. It is only after the fact, as you try to recall what was happening and how it felt... you can begin to see the differences. There is no time, as it is happening to realize it could mean in the reality after combat.

Frankly, the loss I felt for John and Natalia—lasted a nanosecond. Once I heard him shout, "Paul, get outta here, run for it," I didn't think about that loss again, until it was over.

Then I could not stop the tears of what might have been or the laughter for what was.

CHAPTER FIFTY-THREE

O'Neal smiled as he returned and sat down rubbing his dirty hands across his dirty, soot smeared face. "When that fireball hit the air out here it got hot enough to melt down everything that wasn't concrete. That tunnel is sealed tighter than a drum and there wasn't a cook off, no radiation at all. We lucked out, or I should say you did."

Rourke looked up at him from his seat on the ground, Natalia behind him rubbing a cream into the burn on his neck.

I said, "We can put a charge over that mound along the ridge there and bury the missile bunker entrance completely."

John said, "Unless a fault was created on the Night of The War, they wouldn't have built this anywhere near one, it should be safe forever."

"Maybe somebody a thousand years from now will dig it up," I said.

"Perhaps someone a thousand years from now will be too smart to want to," Rourke heard Natalia murmur from behind him.

"A shame our people and your people couldn't have worked together, well, like we did here before... well, before all..." O'Neal said.

"Before the Night of The War," I added somberly, my jacket and shirt gone, my left arm and shoulder heavily bandaged, my eyes glassy from the painkiller Rourke had given me before cleaning and dressing the wound.

"Maybe someday," O'Neal said. Squinting against the afternoon sun, Rourke put on his aviator sunglasses. "Someday, somebody may remember what this place was, maybe build a little marker here, you know?"

Thunder rumbled out of the cloudless sky, the sun blood red. "Maybe someday," Rourke almost whispered. "Maybe."

CHAPTER FIFTY-FOUR

Rourke, Gundersen and I watched as the submarine's deck winch shifted Rourke's Harley, the last of the three bikes to be put onto the rocks. The jet black Harley Low Rider swung precariously from the tackle, then was lowered slowly down.

"How's O'Neal?" Rourke asked.

Gundersen smiled, "Got him in sick bay, got a few more cuts and bruises during that bruha you folks had with Cole and the others. But he's just fine. Told me to give you his best regards, and to wish you luck finding your family."

"Tell him I wish him the same, the best of luck, and if he's looking for someone, to find them, and well, tell him..." Rourke added lamely.

Gundersen laughed. "All right, I'll tell him exactly that."

"Where you bound to?"

"Close as I can get this boat to U.S. II headquarters without a Russian reception committee to welcome me, I guess," Gundersen laughed.

"Then what?"

"Funny talk for a guy who rides around under water, but guess you could say I'm a quote/unquote soldier. I'll follow my orders. Finally got through to U.S. II, ran a radio link through a ham set that opened up last night in Tennessee. Some Resistance people just got onto it, fella named Critchfield. Know him?"

"No. He didn't mention anything about a woman and two children, did he?"

"No, can't say I asked either though, sorry about that."

"I'm heading there anyway, once I get back."

"Well, we made the link," Gundersen said. "Seems Cole was really Thomas Iversenn. He was a National Guard officer, a First Lieutenant. Wandered in one day with about a dozen men or so and volunteered to go regular army."

"They took him. Reed never really trusted him, right wing radical, he called him. U.S. II assigned the real Cole and six men to recover the warheads to use as a bargaining tool against the Soviet Union."

"Somehow, Iversenn found out about it, killed Cole and his men, Reed almost bought it. He took Cole's orders and identity."

"How'd he know so much about the missiles?"

"Worked at the facility that built the warheads; Iversenn had been planning to get to the missiles someday even if there hadn't been a war. Start his own preemptive strike against the Soviet Union and alert Washington to join in or get retaliated against. Crazy."

"Yeah, he was," Rourke nodded, reaching out to the Harley, starting to ease it around as the tackle lowered it. Gundersen and I helped him.

"What about you, John. Reed said he'd like you back. Gave me the coordinates for the new U.S.II headquarters and..."

"I'll memorize the coordinates, just in case I ever need them. But I've got my family to look for, what I was doing before Cole or Iversenn shot Natalia and started this whole thing."

"I'll ask you a favor then, with the jet fighter you've got stashed."

"What's the favor?"

"You said you rigged the ammo dumps and everything at Filmore Air Force base to blow if anyone tampered with it."

"Natalia and Paul did, a good job, I understand."

"This is direct from President Chambers. If the Russians should land forces out here, we don't want them having an airfield to use, or any U.S. material or planes. Could their people debug the stuff Major Tiemerovna and Mr. Rubenstein did?"

"Probably, if they were careful," Rourke answered.

"Then I've got one order for you, order from President Chambers, a request from me."

"I take requests, I don't take orders." Rourke answered softly, easing his bike down and balancing it on the stand.

"Fire a missile into that ammo dump or whatever you need to do to destroy the base completely."

Rourke looked at him, then me and back to the Harley, undoing the binding that held it to the tackle. "All right, I'll make a run on it on the way East. Might not be perfect, but I'll tear up the main runways and hit the ammo dump and arsenal."

"Agreed. I'll tell Reed that, we're talking again before I go under."

Rourke extended his right hand, Gundersen taking it. "Good luck to you, Commander."

"You too, John, maybe we'll see each other again sometime."

Thunder rumbled loudly in the clear morning sky. Rourke didn't answer Gundersen.

CHAPTER FIFTY-FIVE

Rourke had placed the three motorcycles aboard the fighter bomber while Natalia and I—my left arm slung, useless because of the spear wound until it healed—removed as much of the camouflage as necessary.

His plan was to destroy Filmore Air Force base then fly as near the Retreat as possible and get the plane camouflaged once again. He'd go to the Retreat, get the truck, come back for the supplies, leave me to recuperate and read the note Natalia insisted he read, the note from her uncle. If it had been urgent, he said, so much time had elapsed it was not urgent now.

Then regardless of the note, before doing whatever it was General Varakov was so insistent about, he would find his wife, his children; Sarah, Michael and Annie.

But what could Varakov want? I wondered. Perhaps Natalia's position had become untenable and Varakov merely wanted her with him, safe. I had laughed at that, we didn't consider ourselves safe. Witness the recent past.

John said he had made up his mind that whatever it held, the note would not be the important thing. It would be secondary. "I will search Tennessee; search for Resistance units, perhaps someone has seen something of a woman and two children. I wonder if they are still on horseback. Sarah named her horse Tildie. Mine is a big gray with the black mane and tail and four black stockings named Sam. It would be good to ride with them again, to ride Sam, to ride with Sarah."

*****

Rourke maintained radio silence to avoid accidental Soviet detection. He thought static would be unbearable at the higher altitudes anyway. He kept checking his instruments...

Filmore Air Force Base came into view as we came over the ridge of rocks. He adjusted his altitude to match the lower level of the valley floor, beginning the attack run.

"John, if it will be easier," Natalia's voice came through his headset radio, "I can launch the missiles from my controls."

Rourke nodded in his helmet. "No, I'll do it," he told her, his face mask clouding a little as he spoke. He overflew the field, climbing slightly to bank, mentally picking his targets on the computer grids, verifying with the television optical unit mounted under the nose that the base was still untouched and the assault would be necessary.

There were human figures on the ground, wildmen, from the quick look at them. There would be some left, wandering, leaderless.

"Going in," he said into the headset microphone built into his helmet. He poised his left hand over the controls and fired a Phoenix missile. The ammo dump suddenly exploded, a second Phoenix and the armory erupted into a fireball. A cluster of 24 Mk82 580-pound mass iron bombs and the runway was gone... nothing but a crater.

"We're going home," Rourke said quietly.

CHAPTER FIFTY-SIX

Rourke stepped back and surveyed the plane, it was, once again, well camouflaged; but from the air only. To land the craft he had selected the only spot available, and there was little peripheral wooded area nearby to which he could "snuggle" the plane to obscure it at least partially on the ground.

He had made the plane tamperproof, without special parts and equipment, it would be impossible to get it off the ground. He turned, walking toward Natalia and me. I was already straddling my Harley, Natalia standing beside hers; her motor not yet started either.

"Not much more than an hour to the Retreat from here," Rourke called out.

"And then rest for Paul," she said.

"And for you," Rourke told her. "Paul will need those dressings changed at least once a day, he can't do it himself," Rourke told Natalia. "Besides, I have to get moving fast. You're still a little weak from the operation, you know that yourself."

"I am not," she insisted.

"All right, you're not," he smiled straddling the Low Rider.

"Ready?" he asked both of us. I nodded, starting my engine,

Natalia mounted her machine. "Ready," she said, glaring at him. Rourke gunned the Harley ahead, there was a shortcut he thought he could use, taking him through the park that surrounded Anna Ruby Falls outside Helen, Georgia. He aimed the Harley's fork toward it...

*****

"Those shots were from the falls," Rourke almost said, stopping his bike near the top of a hilly rise.

"What do you think, John?" I asked.

"Whatever you want to do," Natalia murmured.

"Can't be too many, not too many shots, sound like assault rifles, but too high pitched for AK-47s, not your people," Rourke said, looking at Natalia.

"Agreed, .223s all of them."

Rourke gunned the Harley. "Let's go!" and let out the machine, starting ahead, up a gully and alongside a row of yearling Georgia pines and then into a sparse woods. Natalia and I roared right behind him.

He hit the top of the rise and bounced a hummock of dirt, slowed the bike, braking, kicking down the stand, dismounting, the CAR-15 in his hands.

Nearing the edge of the falls, he saw three bodies at the bottom of the steep side of the gorge. One on a bridge across the stream at the base of the falls, still another on rocks there beneath the bridge and fifty feet or so beyond. And a third, the third body and the second body still moved.

Men... brigands, moved down from the far side of the gorge, what looked from the distance like M-16s in their hands, five of them. They had not heard the motorcycles coming, I realized, the steady, drowning roar of the falls itself obscuring the noise. I saw the lead man raise his M-16 and fire into the man on the rocks who had moved, the man moved no more.

Rourke shouldered the CAR-15, ripping away the scope covers, flicked the safety, plumping a two shot burst into the lead man. The body fell, Rourke shifting the scope, finding another target, killing. Natalia was taking direct aim with her M-16 and I had my German MP-40, my Schmeisser was spitting rounds, the bodies fell. All five were down. Rourke shifted his rifle, one shot to each man, to each head, five dead.

Natalia said, "John, the one at the base of the grade here, a boy with red hair, he's moving."

Rourke handed her his rifle. "Take the bikes and start along the side here until you can climb down safely, watch your stitches and watch Paul's arm. I'll go this way."

"All right," she whispered.

Rourke started to the edge, found a spot that looked the least steep, and started down, slipping onto his rear end, sliding, catching himself, skidding on the heels of his boots, getting to a standing position, running to keep up with his momentum, slipping, falling back, skidding, then getting his balance.

I found I couldn't make the climb down; my arm just couldn't do it. I told Natalia to go ahead.

Later she told me the boy had died but had been someone that Rourke knew... surprisingly the boy knew someone else and where she was. Sarah.

The boy's name was Bill Mulliner and Sarah, Michael and Annie were at the Cunningham Horse Farm near Mt. Eagle, Tennessee. He had one request, tell his mom he loved her.

Rourke promised he would.

PART THREE

WE KNEW THE END WAS COMING

CHAPTER FIFTY-SEVEN

By this time, Natalia had joined Rourke and the Mulliner boy down at the base of the waterfall, hearing the boy's final words regarding the location of Rourke's family and that they were, at least for the moment, safe. "Oh, my God, Natalia, what happened then?" I asked.

"John stood up, he looked tired, suddenly more tired than I have ever seen him. I said, 'You have found them, John.'"

"Probably," he said, his voice soft, a whisper.

Natalia said, "I told him, that I would go with you to the Retreat and you can help me to unload the cargo from the aircraft and we could get it to the Retreat and I would stay with you until John came back. Then I would go back to Chicago, to my uncle, to the KGB..."

"Crap, what did he say to that?"

"He said, I wasn't leaving... he said I was to stay at the Retreat. Paul, he is so torn, he loves Sarah too, so I told him again that I would leave. He told me he would not let me leave. Paul, God help me... I told him I would stay with him forever if he wanted me and he said yes."

CHAPTER FIFTY-EIGHT

"Do you think, Paul, well, do you think?" Natalia looked at me as we rode along the level grasslands to intersect the highway leading nearest to the Retreat.

When I didn't answer her, she started to raise her voice over the throb of the Harleys' engines, to repeat her question. "Paul, I want to know. What do you..."

I pushed the wire rimmed glasses off the bridge of my nose. "I heard, I just don't know how to answer you. I don't know what to think, to say. I don't know."

Over the sounds of the Harley she said, "You think I'm crazy?" She slowed the Harley under her, arcing it in a wide circle in the grass of the gently rolling field, a house distantly visible, but no sign of human habitation beyond that, and no sign of occupancy.

I slowed my bike, turning in a lazy circle back toward her, and killed my engine. The silence was deafening with both bikes silent.

"What do you want me to say? That I think John should have two wives? Remember, Jews aren't polygamous. And neither are Russians, I hear. So I can't tell you anything more than you know yourself, Natalia."

"But," she looked down at the controls of her machine. "I just, ahh, I don't..."

I smiled, "John wants you to stay, and you want to stay. And for what it matters...," and she watched my eyes behind my glasses. "For what it matters, well, I want you to stay, too. I do."

I broke the background silence gunning my Harley to life. I just looked at her and said, "Ready?" She nodded and we headed back out. We stayed on the road, because it was faster and it was easier on my wounded arm.

A peacefulness seemed to come on her now. John Rourke would find his Sarah, and Michael, and Annie. Whatever was going to be... would be, but I could tell that Natalia Anastasia Tiemerovna, Major, Committee for State Security of the Soviet, felt happiness.

I knew she loved me deeply but it was like she would love a brother, or a close friend. She had had neither. She looked at me as she brushed hair back from her eyes and shouted, "I'm happy, Paul!"

We were starting into a curve as we passed beneath an outstretching road-side oak to our right, the angle of the road dropping steeply left, an abandoned roadside store on the left perhaps forty yards ahead.

In the gravel parking lot between the store and the road were more than a dozen men on motorcycles or standing beside them. Brigands. She swung her M-16 forward on its sling. She slowed her bike and looked at me, my German MP-40 submachine gun was already in my right fist.

I looked sadly at her. It had been foolish, dangerous, to feel happy.

CHAPTER FIFTY-NINE

I laughed when I thought of it, *trigger control*. It had been my slogan, my watchword for so long.

I pumped the Schmeisser's trigger, a neat three-round burst across the forty yards or so separating us from the dozen brigands, pumped the burst toward the nearest of the two brigands raising assault rifles toward us.

A tall, beefy man wearing a sleeveless blue denim jacket doubled up jack-knife fashion, fell forward.

A sharper, louder crack, hot brass pelting at my left cheek, Natalia's M-16, a long burst, the second rifleman going down, his legs cut out from under him.

Gunfire rained down on us now as others of the brigand band opened fire, motorcycles starting out of the gravel parking lot, skidding into the loop of highway that flanked the lot on two sides.

"Back the other way!" Natalia was screaming. I fired another burst, then another and another, the comparatively mild recoil shocking my body, bringing a wash of cold sweat to me, my arm aching like a bad tooth.

I started cutting the Harley into a steep arc, firing another burst, downing still another of the brigand bikers, the brigand's machine, a Japanese bike dripping chrome and gleaming like something just off a showroom floor, skidding across the highway.

The brigand was screaming, dragged behind it, the bike's engine roaring, sparks showering up from the road surface, then a scream more hideous than anything I had ever heard, a shriek.

The brigand's left leg, as the machine whiplashed against a rock of massive proportions, the rock a barrier between the corner of the gravel lot and the loop of highway... was torn away.

The bike exploded as it struck the boulder sized rock, a spray of flaming gasoline belching laterally across the loop of highway then rising. The amputated leg of the brigand was like a flaming log, the brigand himself screaming again as flames engulfed his thrashing body.

I let the Schmeisser drop to my side on its sling, snatching the battered Browning High Power from the web tanker style shoulder rig under my field jacket and jacked back the hammer with my thumb.

I fired once, the brigand biker, a human torch, dropped, the burning arms and hands slapping up toward the face, the face like the burning head of a match. What had been a man fell.

I gunned the Harley, Natalia twenty yards back along the road by now, her machine stopped, the M-16 held in both her hands as she twisted in the bike seat, spraying death behind us.

I shouted, "Run for it!" I shot my machine past her, hearing her machine rev up. I looked behind me; Natalia was coming, riding low over her Harley. Brigand bikers, at least six of them, starting out of the loop of highway and following.

CHAPTER SIXTY

Behind me I heard her M-16 go silent; my machine was weaving, both to avoid brigand gunfire, and because the pain in my arm was making me weak.

There was a roar behind her and I looked back. One of the brigand bikers was breaking away from the rest. He was on a three wheeled trike, the roar of its engine loud.

From what I could tell, it was no real bike at all; it was something customized, hand built, chrome pipes gleaming everywhere, a chrome plated automobile sized engine between the single front and rear wheels, just behind the driver's seat.

There was a rippling, exploding sound, the bike up on its rear wheels for an instant, then rocketing toward us, a cloud of exhaust fumes rising in its wake.

The face of the man driving it, lips wide back from the bared teeth, snarling, one eye gone, the right one. In the left hand, a shotgun, the barrels short, no buttstock at all, as far as I could see.

The double side by side barrels were rising as the three-wheeled machine gained on us. I glanced back and saw Natalia reach her right hand to the Safariland flap holster at her hip, her fingers curling around the smooth, memory grooved Goncalo Alves stocks, the L-Frame Smith & Wesson in her fist as she wrenched it from the leather.

She punched the Metalife Custom .357 Magnum out, toward the man with the shotgun now coming at her on the trike. If he fired first, she would be dead or worse.

The face of the brigand biker seeming to erupt at the bridge of the nose and between the eyes. The shotgun discharged, both barrels, Natalia turned her face away.

She turned to fire again. I saw the trike, the biker and a massive oak tree growing close out of the side of the road... the bizarre machine climbed it, hung from it now as flames rained down in chunks of burning flesh. The trike and the biker... gone.

She holstered the L-Frame and screamed into the wind.

I looked behind us. The brigand bikers had given up their pursuit.

CHAPTER SIXTY-ONE

I didn't know right at that moment, couldn't have known that John was tracking Russian tanks. Ten tanks traveling in column along what had once been an interstate highway.

The tanks were thirty-nine plus ton T-72s, fitted with 125mm smooth bore turret guns, more powerful than anything U.S. II might possibly have to throw against them.

John told me later, "Things would have been alright if they hadn't murdered a stray mother dog and her two pups."

But they had and so John Thomas Rourke settled a debt for a dead momma dog and her pups and killed the man that had killed them. Then all hell broke loose before he had escaped.

CHAPTER SIXTY-TWO

Natalia and I arrived at the Retreat. We were exhausted, but I tried not to show it. I had lost a lot of blood and my arm ached from the wildman's spear.

Natalia stepped into the Retreat behind me. "Welcome home," I told her smiling.

"Paul, why don't I change your bandages, and make you comfortable, there's nothing so heavy that I can't load it into the truck," she said.

"Bullshit, like John'd say. But you can drive the pickup."

She only nodded. We got the truck ready quickly then she forced me to rest on the couch in the Great Room of the Retreat.

I suspect she was hoping against hope that I'd fall asleep. She would've disabled my bike and hers so I couldn't follow her, and I would be forced to rest. But I hadn't fallen asleep and together we got ready to drive away from the Retreat.

The Retreat... John was always prepared, almost. He had not been prepared for her. I thought, whatever happened with Sarah, whatever happened with the world; I felt she would be with John Rourke.

We secured the Retreat doors with their weights and balances locking system, the interior secured with its combination systems.

The truck's lights were out and Natalia drove by the intermittent moonlight. Thunder rumbled, illuminating the high, scattered clouds, the clouds seeming to be a rich blue when lit by the lightning. Beside her, I dozed on and off.

I heard her yawn and roll the window of the camouflage painted Ford pickup truck down, so the cold night breeze would help keep her awake. I heard her mumble a line by the American poet Robert Frost, "...miles to go before I sleep."

Then I slept.

CHAPTER SIXTY-THREE

Natalia stood leaning against the fuselage of the plane, the prototype F-111, only one more crate remained, M-16 rifles. I looked skyward; the horizon was pink tinged, thunder rumbling in the east, streaks of lightning across the pink line between day and night.

I was coming back from the camouflaged Ford pickup and moving like a man twice my age; my left arm stiff at my side.

Natalia turned quickly away from me to the crate of rifles, reaching out for it, drawing it toward her; it was only twenty feet or so to the truck.

"Hey, what the hell are you doin'?" I shouted.

"I'm trying to move the crate, what's it look like, Paul?"

I shoved past her, pain shot through my arm when I made contact with her. My right hand was beside hers on the crate's rope handle, wrenching the crate away from her at an awkward angle.

"I take one end, you take the other, just like we've been doing," I said, not looking at her.

"I can do it, your arm..."

"Bullshit, your abdomen, probably still weak from the surgery, all I need is for you to rupture that area where John operated, now get out."

Her left hand went against my chest as she turned to face me, shoving me back. "All I need is for you to die, get your arm bleeding again. Bullshit to you, too, Paul!"

She was screaming at me. She stopped. I leaned forward, against the fuselage, laughing. Natalia, too, begin to laugh.

"What do you say we just leave this crate of rifles, huh?" I smiled.

"What do you say we just carry it like the other ones, hmm?"

"That's a better idea."

"Yeah, it is a good idea," then I turned to face her fully, and as my right arm moved out to her, she leaned her head against my chest.

"Without your strength, not the physical kind," she said; despite her sex she was my equal in physical stamina and endurance, "life would have been sadder for me."

CHAPTER SIXTY-FOUR

Report from the personal notebook of <u>General Ishmael Varakov</u>, Commander, Soviet Army of Occupation In North America recovered during an archaeological dig at the Field Museum of Natural History, also known as The Field Museum, in Chicago:

I sit on a park bench, halfway across the spit of land extending out into the lake toward the astronomy museum. The wind is stiff and cold off the lake there. Beside me, my secretary Catherine, a shy girl who wears her uniform skirts too long.

A shy girl who had told me that she loved me when I had attempted to send her back to spend the last few days with her mother and her brother in the home I would never again visit beside the Black Sea. She asked me now, "We will all die?"

"Yes, child," I nodded. "We will all die." And thunder rumbled from the sky, a flash of chain lightning snaking low through gray clouds over the white-capped waters of Lake Michigan. The lightning subsided, passed and I whispered to her, "Very soon, Catherine, the lightning will not go away."

She had said it so sweetly. "I will miss it, if you can miss it, Comrade General, being alive, I think."

I looked at her face; the rims of her eyes were moist. "Do you cry child because you die?"

She nodded yes.

"That you die, child? We will all die." She shook her head no. "Why is it that you cry, child?"

"Because I had to be told I would die, die, Comrade General before... before... I..." She looked away from me. She was a virgin. Sensation... it was life and life was right now.

*****

My Reflection:

I had known General Varakov; I had met him with Natalia. I knew him best through her, until his notebook was recovered. I knew him as a soldier, her uncle... the pages of his notebook introduced me to the man.

Chapter Sixty-Five

The camouflaged Ford was parked in the Retreat, the cases of rifles and ammunition and medical gear and other supplies from the aircraft in the truck bed. Natalia was too exhausted to bother moving them and I was too weak.

She had insisted I go to bed, I had insisted on a shower. She had been too tired to argue it with me, so she sat, now, on the floor just outside the bathroom, listening for the sounds of me in the shower.

She was afraid I was too weak to keep standing. She had offered to bathe me and... to tell the truth.... I blushed.

She had smiled; love is a strange thing. I knew her love for me was deep friendship, her love for Rourke something else entirely. But I thought I didn't think she was certain what; then the world went black.

When I came to, my left arm was dripping blood that washed across my naked body on the floor of the shower.

Natalia was stepping into the bathtub, her left hand turning down the shower, her right hand reaching out for me.

My vision was bleary and I slurred a bit as I whispered, "Slipped, I guess, ha," and forced a smile.

"Did you hit your head?" she said leaning over me. As her eyes glanced down, I was coming erect between my legs.

"Get out of here!"

"I'm going to see if you're all right."

"I haven't been this close to..."

"I know," she smiled. "There's nothing to be embarrassed about, it's a normal reaction, you haven't got any clothes on, that's all..."

I laughed, "This is stupid."

"What's stupid?" she said, feeling the back of my head, parting my wet hair to see if I'd injured myself.

"I'm naked in the shower with the most beautiful woman I've ever seen and what am I doing, wishing for an erection to go down because I'm embarrassed."

She kissed my forehead quickly, stepping out of the shower, reaching out to help me to my feet.

"That didn't help me." I smiled... She stopped the bleeding, bandaged my arm after forcing me to let her finish washing me. I thought, *As if any woman could reach maturity and not know what a penis looked like.*

Then she put me to bed, giving me some of the painkiller John had prescribed for me, covering me, turning off the light, and going immediately back into the bathroom. It would need cleaning after the flood from the shower, I knew.

Not yet asleep, I could hear her working, getting up her boot prints, drying the floor. I heard her leave the bathroom; walk down the three steps and into the Great Room.

I heard her light a cigarette. In my mind's eye, I saw her sitting back in the couch, inhaling the smoke deep into her lungs and staring up at the ceiling for a while, the stalactites there reminding her of something she didn't wish to be reminded of.

I saw something else in my mind's eye. On the end table beside the couch was the photograph of John, Sarah, Michael, and Annie.

I thought I heard her say, "What kind of woman are you, Sarah?"

But my eyes were closed and I may have been asleep.

CHAPTER SIXTY-SIX

It would be much later before John would relate this story to me:

John told me he had stopped the Harley Davidson Low Rider, dismounting as he let down the stand.

Below him, in a shallow depression too small to be actually called a valley, was a burned farm house, or so it appeared to be. A barn too, also burned.

There was a white fence, a corral fence, freshly painted it seemed, gleaming white against the blackness of the burned timbers of the two buildings. There was movement near the shell of the house.

It was near Mt. Eagle, it had apparently once been a horse farm. He removed his binoculars from the case with trembling hands. There was a sign, fallen down and broken in half, partially obscured by underbrush. It had been at the end of the dried, mud rutted ranch road, where the ranch road had met the blacktop.

The sign read: Cunningham's Folly Friends Welcome, Others Planted.

As he raised the binoculars to his eyes, focusing them.

"Freeze!"

He froze, whoever was behind him, whoever had spoken, was good, very good.

He told me, "I kept the binoculars at eye level, shifting my right hand slightly so the fingers of my left hand could reach under the storm sleeve of the bomber jacket. With all the Soviet activity, I had hidden the little North American Arms PP4 .22 Magnum boot pistol I'd taken off the dead body of a brigand.

"I had it wrapped by a heavy rubber band, butt downward on the inside of my right wrist. The four-round cylinder was one-round shy, the half-cocked hammer resting over an empty chamber.

"I complimented him on sneaking up on me like that, palmed the little PP4 under my left hand, and kept peering through the binoculars. There was a woman moving about the yard near the white corral fence."

CHAPTER SIXTY-SEVEN

From the pages of <u>General Varakov's</u> notebook, recovered during an archaeological dig at the Field Museum of Natural History, also known as The Field Museum, in Chicago:

I sit at my desk in my office without walls amid the splendors of the museum staring at the mastodons in the distance. Two extinct creatures fighting each other in death.

I have had no further reports of Natalia or of the American Rourke, or of the young Jew who had been with Natalia. It is as if all three had disappeared from the face of the earth.

I have found no trace of Rourke's wife and children either, although I have clandestinely been searching for them for weeks. Partially as further inducement to Rourke, and because I supposed it was the decent thing to do.

Rozhdestvenskiy, Karamatsov's ghost, has succeeded at the Johnson Space Center. My agent inside the KGB verified that he has recovered what was presumed to be the serum and twelve of the American cryogenic chambers.

The American chambers are comparable to our Soviet chambers. It is possible our Soviet chambers can be modified. The serum, if I understand the way of it, would be enough for thousands.

All available army units are being mustered to a central staging area near the Texas/Louisiana border for a final battle with the surviving forces of U.S. II, but not for victory, for slaughter.

I know however, this is a red herring; it is designed simply to keep the army preoccupied, lest the true nature of The Womb be discovered.

I have a small band of trusted GRU and army personnel in place, waiting. They do not know the mission, nor do they know the purpose.

To activate them without my niece and without the American Rourke would be useless. They may not be activated, until the End.

The building is nearly deserted. Some army functionaries, some KGB to keep Rozhdestvenskiy posted as to my actions, but nothing more. Soon, nothing at all.

I sit here watching Catherine as she sleeps curled up in the leather chair beside my desk. She wanted to be with me, because dawn is coming.

But dawn has come and gone and we both live, at least for another day.

My feet hurt; I have not slept or rested much.

CHAPTER SIXTY-EIGHT

Rourke continued, "I said again, there's a woman, young woman, down there by the corral fence. What's her name?' I still got no answer and said, 'I asked her name.'

"I felt the muzzle of a gun at the back of my neck and stepped back against it on my right foot, simultaneously snapping my left foot up and back, hearing a guttural sigh. I felt my heel connect with tissue and bone, my left arm moving as I half dodged, half fell right, sweeping up and against the muzzle of the gun.

"I knocked the barrel of a Ruger Mini-14 stainless aside and the man holding it sagged forward, knees buckling. I told him not to move and that I didn't want to shoot him and I thought we were on the same side. Then again, I asked the name of the woman down by the corral fence.

"The black man looked up, 'Sarah, Sarah Rourke?'"

"I did something I rarely do. I made the sign of the Cross."

CHAPTER SIXTY-NINE

This information was transcribed by <u>Colonel Nehemiah Rozhdestvenskiy</u>, Commander of the North American Branch of The Committee for State Security of the Soviet and discovered at an archaeological dig at the former Cheyenne Mountain complex:

Report # 67200/Personal: I have commandeered a Lear executive jet and am flying to Cheyenne Mountain and The Womb. I have been promoted, my new title is Colonel Nehemiah Gustafus Rozhdestvenskiy, Commander of the North American Branch of The Committee for State Security of the Soviet.

I am meeting Major Revnik, my executive officer. Lodged within what once had been North American Air Defense Headquarters, NORAD is the location of The Womb.

It is guarded by thousands of men and women and tanks, the massive T-72s, plus the generators for our particle beam weapons that form the air defense. That would make us ultimately masters of the earth.

Signed

<original signed>
Nehemiah Rozhdestvenskiy, Colonel. Commander of the North American Branch of The Committee for State Security of the Soviet.

CHAPTER SEVENTY

Natalia told me later that she had sat up all night listening to me breathe and smoking. She finally decided that while she wanted both a shower and sleep, the shower would only serve to keep sleep further out of reach.

She had removed her boots and stretched out on the couch underneath her fur coats, one of the few luxuries she had brought with her from Chicago.

When she woke, she had gone into the bathroom, brushed and flossed her teeth, brushed out her hair. She had stripped and stood under the warm water of the shower.

I slept on until nearly evening; she said she marveled at my kidneys.

Hearing a noise from beyond the closed bathroom door, she had called my name but got no answer. Naked, she stepped out of the shower onto the bath mat, turning down the shower head with her right hand; again she called... still no answer.

She had brought a fresh change of clothes into the bathroom and not a robe. There was no time to get dressed. She wrapped a towel around her. It barely covering her crotch and breasts, grabbing a second towel, she wrapped her soaking wet hair, turban fashion.

She grabbed the two L-Frame .357 Magnum Smiths from the lid of the flush tank and wiped moisture from them and stepped to the bathroom doorway, listening.

More sounds.

Holding one pistol under her left arm, she put her right hand to the doorknob, twisting it open but only slightly ajar.

A sound... the inner door of the Retreat being opened or closed? Not sure which; revolver in each hand, she stepped back from the door and kicked her bare right foot against the door, swinging it outward, fast.

She dropped down onto her right knee, the towel loosening as she moved, starting to slip, both pistols leveled, she searched the Great Room.

A tall, handsome little boy. A pretty little girl with honey-colored hair. John Rourke... visible coming from the storage area to the left of the main entrance and off the great room. A woman.

"Sarah..." The woman was about her own height, pleasant of figure, dark brown hair half obscured by a blue and white bandanna. She stood up.

The woman smiled, but a funny smile. She said, "You must be the Russian woman I've heard so much about..." starting across the Great Room she slowed, then came up the three steps to the level of the bathroom. "I'm Sarah, John's wife," she smiled, standing in front of Natalia. "So you are Natalia."

CHAPTER SEVENTY-ONE

This information was transcribed by <u>Colonel Nehemiah Rozhdestvenskiy</u>, Commander of the North American Branch of The Committee for State Security of the Soviet and discovered at an archaeological dig at the former Cheyenne Mountain complex:

Report # 67201/Personal: The Womb has been refitted to suit both my orders, and my plans. It is no longer recognizable as NORAD Headquarters.

I supervised converting offices into a huge laboratory. I find the bluish glow of the almost luminescent gas that fills one of the twelve American chambers, strangely beautiful.

That idiot, Professor Zlovski, damn his eyes, refuses to verify whether or not the Eden Project serum is working. Apparently there were several types of serum with which Soviet scientists experimented initially, at least some seemed to have the desired effect. When the experiment was concluded, they realized the serums had failed in one aspect or another.

However, according to the data I found, it would seem that scientists both inside and outside the NASA establishment worked with the serum and that the desired results were achieved.

Without a way to accelerate the process, Zlovski insists we are at the mercy of real time here, and there is no way to know until the actual experiment has been performed. In other words, we either won't know for five hundred years, or we will never know.

I may kill Zlovski, damn his eyes.

Signed

<original signed>

Nehemiah Rozhdestvenskiy, Colonel. Commander of the North American Branch of The Committee for State Security of the Soviet.

Chapter Seventy-Two

Natalia, her voice odd-sounding to her, answered, "Sarah, I wanted so to meet you. The children are beautiful."

"So are you."

*****

My arrival broke the tension between the two women. I think John Rourke was so glad to see me, he damned near kissed me. The children adopted me almost immediately and liked Natalia, as well.

Natalia solved the logistical problem at the Retreat because of the addition of three people. "Annie can sleep with me in my room, and Michael can sleep with Paul. That way, you and John can have privacy, it's the best solution," and she had lit a cigarette.

Sarah had said nothing, only nodded agreement.

Annie had been ecstatic, and Michael, a more mature, more low-key child, seemed enthused as well.

After they had explored the Retreat and Rourke had used the microwave to make a hearty dinner that the children liked, there had been showers for Michael and Annie and then both weary children were put to bed.

John and Sarah watched from the doorway; Annie, already asleep in Natalia's room, seemed somehow lost in the king-sized bed. Michael was sleeping as well.

Natalia and I sat on the couch in the Great Room; she in a gray turtleneck knit top and black skirt. I wore blue jeans with my shirt tail out.

Rourke had showered; he wore clean clothes, but clothes identical to what he always wore, except that he was without socks and wore rubber thongs on his feet.

Rourke had provided blue jeans, T-shirts, and sweaters in his wife's size in the stores for the Retreat, as well as underwear and track shoes and two pairs of combat boots.

Sarah wore clothes Natalia had practically insisted that she borrow. "Sarah would feel more at ease in more normal clothes." A pale blue blouse, Sarah had added a blue A-line skirt. And since the temperature in the Retreat seemed cold to her, Sarah had added a navy-blue cardigan sweater.

Incongruously, she wore a pair of the rubber thongs he had stockpiled for her, black soled and not matching the rest of what she wore at all. "What's the matter?" Sarah asked him.

"Just looking at you, it's good to be able to say that, just looking at you."

"I suppose I can always let Natalia borrow one of the three dozen pairs of Levis you stored here for me."

"I didn't know what to buy for you, you'd never even come up here."

"I'm not blaming you," she smiled.

He let out a long sigh. "What do you say I buy you a drink, huh?"

"All right," and he watched the little dimples at the corners of her mouth deepen as she smiled up at him. "All right, I'd like that."

The acoustics in the Great Room were so good that I could still hear their hushed conversation. "Thanks for trying so hard, I mean Natalia seems like a good person, and I like Paul. But Natalia's in love with you, you know that, don't you? And you're in love with her.

"I didn't say you weren't in love with me, I know you are. I knew that wouldn't change. You love us both. And she knows that and so do I. Do you have any idea what's going to happen, to the three of us?" She leaned her head against his right shoulder, Rourke holding her left hand.

"You're my wife and..."

"I know a lot about you, John, I always did. Sometimes, before The Night of the War, sometimes a friend would intimate that you were fooling around when you were away from me on those trips..."

"I never."

"I always knew that, I never questioned it. Whatever happened between you and Natalia just happened, I guess that's why I can't be mad at her, either. I wouldn't have blamed you if you had, the children and I could have been dead. You looking for us like you did, finally finding us, that's an act of love no one in her right mind could argue with, dispute."

"It was something I didn't prepare for, do you know?"

"I know," and she leaned up to kiss him lightly on the mouth. "Let's sit down, Natalia has that letter from her uncle that she wanted us to hear and you promised me a drink, we can't settle anything now."

Rourke took her in his arms, kissing her hard.

CHAPTER SEVENTY-THREE

We all sipped at a glasses of Seagram's Seven and ice; Rourke smoked one of his thin, dark tobacco cigars, Natalia smoked a cigarette on the couch between me and Sarah.

John sat in the reclining chair that flanked the coffee table opposite the couch. Natalia handed him an envelope. "It is addressed to you, John." He nodded, leaning forward, taking the envelope, his fingers touching hers as he took it.

Rourke sipped again at his drink. He looked at Sarah, "Natalia's uncle is General Ishmael Varakov, he's the supreme commander for the Soviet Army of Occupation in North America, but he's been straight with me the times I've had dealings with him.

"He's the head of the bad guys, you might say," and his eyes flickered to Natalia, watching the muscles at the corners of her blue eyes tighten slightly, "but an honorable man. He's a soldier doing his job; a patriotic Russian... can't fault him for that."

And then Rourke looked at the letter. It was dated some four weeks earlier. He began to read, out loud.

"Doctor Rourke, If you read this letter, Natalia, my niece, has arrived safely to your care. You may wonder that my English is so good; I spent many years in Egypt and in order to understand as much as I could, it was necessary to improve what English I already knew or master Arabic, the Egyptian variant, precisely.

"I had dealt with American and British officers during World War II and spoke English well enough to make myself understood, so I polished my

English. I have sent Natalia to you not only for the reason which you suspect, that her position here deteriorates, as does mine. But another, more grave reason.

"You have heard, I'm sure, at least casual reference to something called The Eden Project, an American project done in cooperation with the NATO, SEATO, and Pan-American allies, but not with their full knowledge. It was a counter-measure to a post thermonuclear holocaust scenario, and this scenario is unfortunately coming to pass. When it transpires, very soon now, few if any living things will survive.

"What I offer to you, to the young Jew Rubenstein, and to your wife and children should you have located them by now, or find them still, is the slim hope of survival. It will in no way compromise your beliefs as a capitalist, nor my beliefs as a communist, if either dialectic can even matter.

"I offer this in exchange for your continued care of my niece, Natalia, like a daughter to me she has been all these years. I helped to raise her as the child of my dead brother and his wife, my brother a physician of great renown, his wife a prima ballerina.

"I assume that you read this aloud to Natalia, if such is the case, help her to understand me when she learns this. For I had no brother at all, only two sisters who died during the early days of World War II. Natalia's father was indeed a physician of some great renown...,"

Rourke looked up; Natalia was staring, saying nothing, her eyes fixed, "but a Jew. Her mother indeed was a ballerina, of the most incredible beauty and grace, her background Christian, and she was a practitioner of this religion despite the numerous injunctions of the State."

Rourke looked at Natalia again.

I sat next to her and held her left hand in my right.

"I was deeply in love with Natalia's mother, her name was Natalia too. But I learned the original Natalia who was as honest and decent a woman as is my Natalia, my niece, that she had secretly married Dr. Carl Morovitch, the Jewish physician.

"Considering myself a gentleman, I withdrew. But it was some years after the War, World War II, that Morovitch, himself only half Jewish, his mother's family name Tiemerov, spoke out against the oppression of Jews in the Soviet Union. I learned through my sources in GRU that his wife, Natalia, the woman I had loved, had departed the ballet before Morovitch's rash actions, which, had she been associated with them, would have forced her expulsion. And that Natalia was pregnant.

"I learned also that the KGB was plotting against Morovitch. I endeavored to warn Morovitch and Natalia, I still loved her, and she knew that I did. But they could not escape because Natalia was due to deliver her child. The child was born, a girl, long legged and skinny, but with eyes the most beautiful blue color I had ever seen, except for the eyes of her mother.

"It was the father of my dead chauffeur, Leon, who accompanied me that night to the home outside Moscow where Morovitch and Natalia and the newborn child were in hiding from the KGB. Leon's father and I went there, because, through my GRU contacts, I knew the KGB was alert to their whereabouts.

"It was our intent, Leon's father was as loyal to me as Leon himself..., to spirit them away and get them to Finland and then to Sweden where they would be safe. We arrived too late..."

Rourke looked up, relighting his cigar, Natalia was weeping, Sarah's left arm around her shoulders. Rourke took a good swallow of his drink. "...to save them. Doctor Morovitch had owned a gun; I had given it to him. He resisted the KGB as I too would have done. To defend his family. Carl Morovitch was dead, shot three times in the chest, then his throat slit. Natalia was bleeding and dying, one of the KGB officers was attempting to rape her.

"I shot him in the head, and then general shooting began. Leon's father was killed defending the small room Morovitch and Natalia had used as a nursery for the baby girl. I was shot in the leg, the left leg, and I still carry the bullet there.

"I could not trust a doctor to remove it at the time, and afterwards it became physically impossible to remove. But all the KGB were dead. The infant girl still lived. There was a woman, also once a dancer, whose services I used from time to time and whose discretion I trusted. I brought the infant to her. Through those few persons I trusted, with meticulous care, I altered my army records to indicate a brother who had lived with relatives ever since birth. This because of my family's poverty.

"I was a general by then, and the task was not as difficult as might be imagined. I found in recent death records a doctor who had no known family, a doctor named Plenko. It was not uncommon in the Twenties and Thirties to change one's name in Russia; it was sometimes a necessity to disguise criminal background or unfavorable political association. I made this man my brother. I invented of whole cloth a woman who was secretly his wife, but the name uncertain, and I invented her death.

"This too was simple enough. With parents for the infant girl, and myself established as her uncle, I acquired the house I still own, on the Black Sea, ensconcing the trusted woman there as my housekeeper and to raise Natalia during my absence.

"For that is what I named her, Natalia, after her beloved, exquisite mother. The eyes gave me no choice, nor did my heart. And then Anastasia, because to me she was the lost princess, thought dead. But my Anastasia was alive. And Tiemerovna after her father's family.

"Years later, the woman who was caring for Natalia married a doctor, his name Tiemerovitch, perhaps some distant relative of Morovitch's family. The woman and Tiemerovitch loved Natalia as their own. I once again altered my background records, eliminating the references to Dr. Plenko and instead linking Dr. Tiemerovitch to myself as a lost brother. Tiemerovitch's medical career was greatly enhanced by the newly 'discovered' relationship to a prominent Soviet general. I lied to Natalia only in that her 'father' was my brother. Her father and mother, Tiemerovitch and his wife, died in an accident when Natalia was eighteen. Again I took her in and saw to it that she had the best education, the best training.

"When she saw her patriotic duty as being linked to the KGB, I did not dare to interfere lest something somehow be suspected and in times such as these, perhaps the greatest safety lies in being counted among those who threaten the safety of others.

"When she married Karamatsov, I was disheartened, but saw it as further enhancing her safety. Natalia, my niece, is all that I have; my obsession is that she live. Her mother died at the same age Natalia is now. I do not wish this for Natalia, whom I love.

"There is a choice for you. To save yourself, your friend, perhaps your wife and children, and since we both love her so deeply..."

Rourke licked his lips, looking at his wife, then looking at Natalia. He finished the letter, repeating the last few words, "... and since we both love her so deeply, my niece. You must come to me in Chicago before it is too late and bring Natalia with you, for there is no other way of it than to force her into danger again. I offer you the chance at life against certain death. Look to the skies, the electrical activity there each dawn, the End is coming."

A scrawled signature was at the bottom of the note; the note itself was printed by hand. Rourke folded the pages of the note together, setting down his cigar.

Natalia, her voice like we had never heard it, stood up, her fingers splayed along her thighs. "I will change to suitable clothes, my uncle..."

Rourke smiled at her, stood, walked around the table and folded her into his arms. "He loves you, and God help me, so do I. We'll leave as soon as you've changed." Still holding Natalia, he looked at Sarah's eyes. After all the years of marriage, the years of arguing, there was no argument there, but the understanding he had sought for so long.

CHAPTER SEVENTY-FOUR

John's weapons were laid out, his gear ready. He and Natalia would ride double on his Low Rider to the place where they had left the prototype F-111, using that to get them to Chicago, it was the fastest way.

Sarah stood behind him; he could feel her hands on his shoulders. He bent over to kiss Annie, "I love you, honey, honest," he whispered to her. She rolled over, not awakening, but a smile crossing her lips.

They left Natalia's room, Annie sleeping there, and moved on to Paul's room, Michael.

Rourke sat again on the edge of the bed. He looked at his son. He spoke to his wife. "If I die, Paul will care for you and the children. And pretty soon Michael will help him. Maybe he's too much like me..."

"He is," Sarah's voice murmured in the darkness.

"I tried," Rourke whispered, sighing loudly. "Honest to God, I tried. To be a father, a husband. If General Varakov is right, hell..." and he bent his head over his son, crying.

Sarah held his head, and in the darkness, she whispered, "I'll always love you, I hate your guts, but I'll always love you. I'll be with you if we all live or if we all die."

He swallowed hard, hugging his wife to him, and he let himself cry because he might never come home again...

*****

I helped John buckle on his gear, the old holster rig for the Python. The belt was heavier, a spare magazine pouch with two extra-length eight shot magazines for his .45s, the magazines made by Detonics. The belt also held the black-handled Gerber Mk II fighting knife with double-edged stainless blade with saw teeth near the double-quillon guard on each side.

He had the little Metalifed Colt Lawman in a special holster made by Thad Rybka for him years before The Night of The War; it carried the gun in the small of his back at a sharp angle.

He picked up the Government Model .45, a Mk IV Series '70, like the other two Colts he carried, was Metalifed. He rammed it into his trouser band.

He wore the twin stainless Detonics .45s in the shoulder rig from Alessi, and the little Russell black Chrome Sting lA was on his belt. The CAR-15 lay on the kitchen countertop. Beside it an M-16, one he had taken the time to handpick from the stores of weapons brought from the plane. Between the two assault rifles was an olive drab ammo box, eight hundred rounds of 5.56mm Ball. Rourke lit a cigar, and glanced at me; I was tired and worn from loss of blood. Rourke had inspected the wound, there had been little progress, almost none, but it was healing.

"I still say..." I started.

Rourke looked at me, "No. With that wound, well... you know. But even if you didn't have the wound, I'd leave you here. Who the hell is gonna take care of Sarah and Michael and Annie for me? There's no one else I'd trust if there were somebody else around."

"So it's you and Natalia against whatever the hell her uncle's throwing you at?"

"Yeah, I guess that's the way of it."

"If you..."

"Don't come back, I can't tell you what to do. You're the best friend I ever had, in some ways, I guess, maybe the only one... I have faith in you, I really do," and Rourke looked at me and smiled...

Natalia appeared wearing what I considered her battle gear, a tight-fitting black jump suit, nearly knee-high medium-heeled boots, the double-flap holster rig on her belt with the L-Frame Smiths bearing the American Eagles engraved on the barrel flats. She opened each holster in turn and checked the cylinders, then reholstered and secured the holster flaps.

As she walked across the Great Room, the COP Derringer was not to be seen, the little four barreled .357 Magnum would be in her massive black canvas bag. On her belt was a Gerber Mk II, the sheath apparently specially made, black, efficient looking, the knife's handle material and the brass double-quillon guard betraying it as the Presentation series variation, just as efficient as the more subdued looking Gerber Rourke wore, but prettier.

She wore a shoulder rig I had never seen before, not something designed for concealment, but a field rig. Under her right armpit was what I guessed was a Gerber Guardian. Black-handled and hanging upside down in a black leather sheath it was similar in size to John's Sting lA.

Under her left armpit, balancing the rig, was a stainless steel Walther PPK/S, hanging upside down like the knife, protruding through the upside of the holster what could have been some type of aluminum silencer, perhaps six inches long and the approximate diameter of a silver dollar.

She saw me looking at it. "I had the silencer specially built, aircraft aluminum but very strong. The baffles need changing after every five hundred rounds or so, there's no slide lock, but I had the recoil spring altered so it functions perfectly with subsonic ammunition. It's very quiet that way, almost like a whisper.

"With the regular recoil spring I have in it now, it handles 95-grain Hollow Points and it sounds about like a belch. I tested it a lot, but never used it in the field. In case we need a relatively silent shot, this should do it."

John saw Sarah looking at him, she stood beside Natalia. He walked over to the two women, his right arm around Sarah, his left around Natalia. He drew both women close. There was no need to say what he felt.

CHAPTER SEVENTY-FIVE

Sarah Rourke fixed drinks for the two of us, Seagram's Seven and ice and a drink for herself. John's taste in liquor was... well, if someone at the Retreat didn't like his favorite blended whiskey ... they were out of luck.

"Good thing you're not a Scotch drinker," she called out to me, forcing a smile.

"Yeah, good thing," I nodded.

I was sitting on the sofa in the Great Room as she brought my drink and her own; she sipped at hers briefly, studying the kitchen. "A microwave oven, God... It will be good to really cook again."

She walked down into the Great Room, sat my drink in front of me on a coaster on the coffee table and then sat down at the farthest corner of the couch from me. Tucking her legs up under her, she tugged at her borrowed skirt, smoothing it over her thighs.

I wondered if she thought about the woman it belonged to; the woman who rode with her husband through the night, to do something or other that Sarah might not quite understand.

She sipped at her drink again. "Is there something wrong?"

I looked at her, pushing my wire-rimmed glasses up on the bridge of my nose. "No, Mrs. Rourke."

"It's Sarah, Paul. Call me Sarah, please."

"Sarah," I nodded, picking up my drink, taking a swallow of it.

"There's something bothering you, is it that John left you here to stay with us and..."

"He couldn't have taken me the way my arm is, no. That just happened. It's not his fault, so I guess..."

"But there's something bothering you," she insisted. As she moved her right hand, setting her drink down on a coaster on the end table nearest her, she saw the picture of herself and the children on the far side of the couch.

"I gotta talk, I shouldn't, ahh..." and I exhaled loudly, too loudly. It was as though something were bottled up inside me, just about to escape.

She smiled. "I just realized... this is the first time in a long, long time I'm not wearing a gun." She wasn't wearing a gun, she was wearing a skirt. She sat in a secure place on a comfortable couch. "I think we're going to be friends, Paul, the children really seemed to take to you. And I think, well, I think, so do I, you can tell me. Sometimes just telling somebody is..."

I stood up, too quickly, pain shooting through my left arm as I walked behind the couch and stood beside the glass front gun case, there were empty spots in the case now. I started. "Before I met your husband," my voice sounded slightly breathless, pain perhaps, but maybe not my arm. And my words were very hurried. "I was just riding a desk in New York City. I had a girl, but New York isn't there anymore and neither is she. And I guess, shit..." I turned around and stared at her, my eyes wide. "If what Natalia's uncle talked about is right, and maybe the world ends but somehow we just go right on living, what the hell am..." I turned away, I bit my lip.

"You'll be lonely, no girl left for you," she whispered. "I know that feeling, Paul. John has me and he has Natalia and you have no one."

I realized at that moment this was a very smart woman, I looked back at her, saying nothing.

*****

My Reflection:

What I had thought would be the end of our journey simply proved to be the beginning of another. But I get ahead of myself.

The meeting between Sarah and Natalia was... awkward and tense to say the least. John Rourke was... just PLAIN uncomfortable. Wrong word, I don't know how to explain how John was and I doubt he could put it into words. Things were moving too quickly to have the luxury of assessment. I was overwhelmed with experiencing, observing, anticipating, guessing... all of these things and more. It was very confusing.

Then before anything of substance was settled, John and Natalia left and I was left behind as the "man of the house" with Sarah and the kids. I had been searching for Sarah and the kids for all of this time... not knowing who they really were or how they felt. Then suddenly... here they were. Sarah was exactly what I had pictured... except she wasn't. She was more.

Michael and Annie, just kids... but now kids destined to be forever in the rest of my life and I had no idea how. Wow... CRAZY!!!

CHAPTER SEVENTY-SIX

Transcribed from a series of interviews with John Rourke. <u>John Rourke is speaking unless otherwise indicated:</u>

We landed at a small country airstrip; the runway in good shape, and the small airfield just north of the Illinois, Wisconsin line was the closest thing my map had shown and small enough, I hoped would have no Soviet guards.

Things seemed alright until... we ran into Tom Maus, Morris Dombrowski and Emily Bronkiewicz, the Combined Counties Resistance Fighters and some Russians.

Natalia was recognized by the Resistance fighters as having been seen with General Varakov.

I'm going to make a very long and very bloody story a little shorter. We aligned with the Resistance and killed a bunch of the Russians. Later we faced brigands, sex crazed cannibals and more Russians.

Natalia and I had been rescued by a Captain Vladov, of the Russian Special Forces, and taken to General Ishmael Varakov.

Inside the entrance to the museum were two fighting mastodons dominating the central hallway. At the far side of the chamber, sixty feet away, stood Varakov, Natalia's uncle. Huge in his bulk, but of average height, his face was a combination of sternness and the warmth of a homeless dog. His uniform tunic open, his feet moving as though it hurt him to stand.

Moving to the Egyptian area, Varakov sat on a backless low wooden bench, Natalia rushed to huddle beside him, for all the world looking like an overly tall little girl. General Varakov at last spoke. "There is little time, perhaps no time at all, but only God, if indeed there is one, can determine that now."

A woman joined us, she was slightly built, what most men would call plain, but there was a prettiness about her. She walked over to stand beside and slightly behind Varakov, the bench separating them. She was Catherine, his secretary, but she was also much more to the older man I sensed. Her right hand came to rest for a second on his right shoulder, lovingly, I thought, then moved away, and folded inside her left hand.

Varakov told Captain Vladov that Natalia and I would be going to Colorado to The Womb and he and his Special Forces were to accompany us. "Yes, Comrade General," Vladov answered. Then began the most important conversation of my life, every word imprinted indelibly on my mind.

Varakov turned to Natalia, "Child, what does ionization of the atmosphere mean to you? You were very bright at the polytechnic, so tell this to me."

"The air, it would become charged with electrical particles, and..."

"When the sun heated it," I interrupted, "the electrically charged particles would..."

"You are correct, both of you. I had little education; it took me a great deal of time to grasp this idea. But soon, all will understand it."

"You alluded to the end of the world," I said.

"In the Judeo-Christian Bible, I believe that God promises this man who built the big ship that the world would never again end by water flooding it over, but by fire instead."

"I always thought that was a poor bargain on Noah's part," I said. "I'd rather drown, I think, than burn to death."

"But it will be swift, Dr. Rourke, so very swift."

"Total ionization of the atmosphere," I murmured.

"Yes, the end of the world. It is coming, a few hours, a few days... but it should be complete within five days at the most. It will come at dawn, rolling through the sky, fire, consuming everything, the very air that we breathe, purging the Earth, sweeping the entire planet. There should be no air to breathe for at least three hundred years, nearer five hundred years before the oxygen content would be able to sustain higher life forms without special breathing apparatus. We have destroyed ourselves, finally and irretrievably... all mankind shall perish from the Earth forever."

"The Eden Project," Varakov said slowly. "With the ionization would come the complete destruction of breathable atmosphere, at the lowest elevations the air thinner afterward than on the highest mountains. The partial destruction of the ozone layer at the very least. All of this was a postwar scenario, one of many. For a time, it was like a guessing game, this War of Wars."

"Einstein," I murmured. "Once he told a questioner that he didn't know what the weapons of World War III would be but that World War IV would be fought with rocks and clubs."

"World War IV, that is why I have called you here, Dr. Rourke. Your sheer survival, your background, you are like the men in the Russian fairy tales who rode the horses of power and fought evil. My niece, she is consummate in her skills at destruction, yet both of you are human beings, have experienced love, for each other and others. Captain Vladov here, he is, to my reckoning, the finest soldier in the Soviet Army..."

"Comrade General, I..." Vladov was embarrassed, but pride gleamed in his eyes again.

"I have found a small cadre of GRU and army personnel whom I can trust. I would advise, perhaps, that you contact U.S. II headquarters through the Resistance, and perhaps they can send forces to aid all of you.

"Otherwise, the only ones who will survive the last sunrise are two thousand men and women handpicked by Rozhdestvenskiy, ones your husband...," he looked at Natalia, "had selected, the list only slightly altered after Rozhdestvenskiy took over his position here. One thousand of the KGB Elite Corps, one thousand women from all branches of service, a staff of doctors, scientists, researchers, three thousand in all, perhaps a few less. They will inherit the Earth if you do not act."

"You mentioned the Eden Project, Uncle Ishmael," Natalia almost whispered.

The old man nodded. "Post holocaust scenarios, guessing games. An Ark was built, that is the Eden Project, my children, an Ark. If Rozhdestvenskiy and his KGB Elite Corps survive in The Womb of theirs in Cheyenne Mountain, your NORAD headquarters before The Night of The War, they will use these particle beam weapons to destroy the six returning space shuttles five hundred years from now, to destroy the last survivors of the human race except themselves, so they will be masters of the new Earth."

I watched General Varakov's eyes, the light of reason in them, not hatred or jealousy or fear. I realized I sat at the feet of greatness. "Your scientists and ours, for many years have attempted to solve the mysteries of cryogenic sleep for use in deep space travel and exploration. But, if the subject could be placed in suspended animation deeply enough to retard the aging process, it was too deep for the brain to be revived.

"The United States cracked the right chemical codes and developed a serum which, once injected into the subject artificially, induced the deep sleep of cryogenic freezing before the actual freezing process took hold. This allowed the brain wave patterns of the subjects to stay at sufficient levels that the subjects could be aroused from their sleep.

"Utilizing the pressurized cargo bays of the space shuttles, it was your own Dr. Chambers, your de facto President, who was largely responsible for the plan. An international corps of one hundred twenty of the finest and best astronaut trainees was assembled, of all races, from all nations of the NATO, SEATO and Pan American Alliances, all nations of the world except the Soviet Union and The Warsaw Pact nations.

"They were trained arduously, the healthiest and brightest, the most skilled and most talented... they never knew their real purpose. They launched on The Night of The War. One hundred twenty souls, plus the six, three-man crews. A cargo bay that held microfilm of all the world's greatest learning, greatest literature, sound libraries of music, video libraries detailing medical techniques, construction techniques, cryogenically frozen embryonic animals and fish and birds, an Ark. That is the Eden Project, they launched just before the missiles destroyed the Kennedy Space Center.

"Presumably they are out there, on an elliptical orbit that will take them to the very edge of the solar system and then return them to Earth in five hundred and two years. Rozhdestvenskiy and his KGB Elite Corps prepare themselves for the cryogenic sleep, to awaken in five hundred years and destroy the Eden Project when it returns.

"What I offer you, Dr. John Rourke, is the hope that you and your wife and children will survive this final holocaust. Twelve of the American cryogenic sleep chambers were taken from an underground laboratory in Texas. Along with these, dozens of jars, we know not exactly how much of the cryogenic serum that prevents the brain death of the subject.

"Go to Colorado, steal back this serum, what you need for your family and yourself and your friend Rubenstein... and for Natalia, I beg that. Steal however many of the cryogenic chambers your airtight Retreat Natalia speaks of, will support. Save yourself, save Natalia, save your family, perhaps these men as well," he gestured toward Vladov. "But above all, destroy The Womb; rob Rozhdestvenskiy of the cryogenic serum, otherwise, all the light of humanity will be extinguished in evil forever."

CHAPTER SEVENTY-SEVEN

Transcribed from historical artifacts of the government of U.S. II located in an archaeological dig, in an area formerly identified as Texas:

President Chambers saw the MiG 27s closing from the horizon line to the east and shouted to his driver, "Get this thing going faster!"

The MiGs screamed through the air above, machine gun fire chewing chunks out of the road surface as the MiGs attacked the U.S. II defensive position.

Chambers realized suddenly, driving in a Volkswagen down an otherwise deserted road toward U.S. II lines the MiGs would have had no way of knowing he was the president and no desire to waste a missile to destroy him.

"Where is Lieutenant Feltcher and the TVM? Did he ever reach the Texas Volunteer Militia at all?" Sam Chambers did not to expect a miracle but he closed his eyes and prayed for one anyway.

CHAPTER SEVENTY-EIGHT

My Reflection:

This part of the adventures of the Rourke family is just as complex as the last one was... maybe even more so.

It was not until I actually sat down and began working on this part of the story that I realized how much was going on simultaneously in so many different locations and realities and experiences.

The sheer complexity of the events in this chapter requires special handling. There were still a multitude of events that were transpiring outside of my awareness that are absolutely integral for you, the reader, being able to comprehend the totality of what was occurring.

Again much of this information has been gleaned from interviews shortly after the events they described; some long after the fact. As before, this is supplemented by the archival records from the Russians, particularly General Ishmael Varakov and some of his subordinates within the Soviet Army of Occupation in North America, discovered long after The Night of the War.

Looking back from the perspective of time, it was easy to forget how these sequences of events changed and became relevant to the fabric of this tapestry that was woven for the Rourke family.

Please bear with me a bit; had I known how hard it would be to relive this... had I known how much these memories would affect me... had I known how the pain of loss and fear and indecision would come back to me... as fresh and damnable as it was in those moments so long ago...

I would have never written the first word.

PART FOUR

THE HEAT OF EARTH FIRE

CHAPTER SEVENTY-NINE

Excerpts from an After Action Report by Colonel Reed, U.S. II, Chief of Intelligence, and a conversation he had with John Rourke. <u>Colonel Reed is speaking unless otherwise indicated:</u>

I jumped from the Jeep before it had fully stopped and shouted to my driver, "Get up the road to the high school and warn headquarters and tell 'em to pull out fast and to use Emergency Plan Three, got that, Corporal?"

I ran toward the grammar school building that had been converted to a field hospital; the wounded needed to be evacuated before the Soviet choppers struck. I hit the steps, taking them three at a time.

The guard just inside the door was clambering to his feet, getting his rifle up to present arms, I snarled, "Can it, Soldier, get to the administrator's office, fast... tell him we're evacuating, we're using Emergency Plan Three, on the double..."

Running past the doors and into the main corridor, I saw classrooms converted to laboratories and wards, the largest of the wards the lunchroom itself. I ran to one of the smaller wards, it housed the few female patients being treated.

I ran shouting, "We're evacuating; Soviet Air Cavalry unit five minutes out, maybe six. Get these patients ready to travel!"

"But..."

"No buts, do it," I said sprinting on to the end of the corridor toward a nurse. "Nurse, start getting the patients ready. We're movin' out fast, Russian choppers five or six minutes out!"

Not waiting for an answer, I ran toward what had been one of the kinder-garten rooms, it held only one bed. A white-haired woman laid in it, sitting on the edge of the bed beside her was a white-haired man. The man's face looked carved from stone, pain etched around the eyes, the jaw set.

An IV tube ran between a half empty bottle and the woman's arm. The man stood up. "Colonel Reed."

I saluted, despite the tattered civilian clothes the man wore rather than a uniform. "Sir, there's a Soviet Air Cav Unit on the way, we don't have much time. Your wife, Sir, she has to be moved."

The older man's eyes flickered. "Colonel Reed, you're active duty; I'm just a retired Air Force officer. This is your show. But she can't be moved, you move the other ones, Colonel. My wife stays here and... And I stay with her."

"Sir..."

"She's dying, she knows it and I know it. I'm not going to take the last few hours she might have left away from her. If the Russians come, then maybe we'll both die together."

I shook my head. "No, no... what about your son?"

"He would understand, Colonel."

I shook my head again. "No, he wouldn't. If I were your son, I wouldn't understand. You've got an obligation to live, Sir. Your wife'd be the first one to tell you that..."

"That's enough Colonel, get out of here, let my wife die in peace and may-be me with her. Cancer will probably get her before the Russians, son." The older man smiled. "Go."

I balled my fists together along the outside seams of my fatigues, I nodded at the older man... my friend. I stepped into the corridor. "Shit," I snarled, hammering my fist against the wall. "Damnit to hell!"

My own mother had died of cancer and now another mother was doing the same and I couldn't do a damn thing about it.

Running back along the bend in the corridor, I heard the voice of the hospi-tal administrator announcing the evacuation over the intercom. "There is nothing to fear, maintain order."

I thought, *Bullshit, since the Night of The War, there had been nothing but fear. Fear that that the War would never end, fear that the Russians could never be displaced from the power they had seized in North America, fear that the guy you shared a smoke with was someone you'd never see again.*

After the evacuation of the Florida peninsula before the mega quake that severed it from the continental U.S., I had come to think of this older man and his wife like a second set of parents. I had suffered with them both when it had been learned she was dying of bone cancer and that nothing could be done to save her.

I had accepted her death as inevitable, but not the death of her husband who had become my close, very close friend.

I reached the end of the corridor, starting to thread my way through the evacuees and toward the doors leading to the outside. I checked my watch; the Russian gunships would fill the skies at any moment. I jerked the Colt .45 from its battered flap holster, worked the slide, jacking a round into the chamber, leaving the hammer at full stand and upped the safety.

I reached the outer doors; the guard there was directing the flow of traffic, wheelchair patients to the ramp, ambulatory patients down the steps. Above the shouts and the blaring of the PA system, I heard the thrashing noise in the air. I could see their outlines, like a swarm of mechanical locusts coming to devour all in their path.

I shouted toward the sky, toward the Soviet force, "God damn you all to hell!" I shot a glance over my shoulder, the older man; my friend was standing in the window watching. In his hand, a .45 caliber Colt Officer's model, the older man raised the window.

"Colonel Reed, if you see my son. Tell him his mother and I love him and we were together at the end."

"I will, Colonel Rubenstein. I promise to do my best to find Paul and tell him." I saluted and ran for the jeep.

*****

My Reflection:

I knew my parents loved each other. I knew they had died together but not how. When I learned the details... my heart was broken. Then strangely a warmth crept over me. "... his mother and I love him and we were together at the end."

Thirteen words to heal a heart; God's grace is an amazing thing.

Chapter eighty

This information was transcribed by <u>Colonel Nehemiah Rozhdestvenskiy</u>, Commander of the North American Branch of The Committee for State Security of the Soviet and discovered at an archaeological dig at the former Cheyenne Mountain complex:

Report # 67203/ Personal: I have been directly involved with the testing of the cryogenic chambers. I have found the coffin shaped object's blue light seems to flicker. The swirling clouds inside it parting, as did clouds before the dawn.

I find this prophetic, in a very real way. I consider it is a dawn, the dawn of a new age for Earth... if I survive.

Zlovski, that imbecile... damn his eyes.

His chin trembles ever so slightly from the oscillation of the spear point of his little beard. He has altered our Soviet made chambers so they match function for function those twelve chambers of American manufacture which I confiscated from the ruins of the Johnson Space Center along with the ninety-six three liter bottles of the nearly clear green liquid, the all important serum.

The name of Corporal Vassily Gurienko has been added to the list of courageous heroes, he was injected with the cryogenic serum; luckily in the correctly calculated amount of the cryogenic serum based upon body weight. When he awoke from suspended animation, I personally conducted tests to ensure that physically and mentally Gurienko was unaltered.

The cryogenic chambers must be able to carry ourselves, those of us on the Committee For State Security Elite Corps and the selected female comrades and the support personnel, five hundred years into the future to reawaken... to reawaken to conquer the planet and to destroy the six returning United States Space Shuttles with our particle beam defense systems before they are able to land.

Professor Zlovski, damn his eyes, still postulates "...there is no proper test of so short a duration and he, Gurienko, must be subjected to extensive medical tests before we know more."

Damn his eyes! I have ordered the Communications Section to send a coded signal to the Kremlin Bunker and to continue sending until there is response. The message contains only one word. "Come."

I find myself in a remarkable state of peace, almost sublime. Like the gods of Greco-Roman myth, I am immortal now.

Signed

<original signed>

Nehemiah Rozhdestvenskiy, Colonel. Commander of the North American Branch of The Committee for State Security of the Soviet.

CHAPTER EIGHTY-ONE

Transcribed from a series of interviews with John Rourke and myself.
<u>**John Rourke is speaking unless otherwise indicated:**</u>

General Ishmael Varakov sat on his backless bench, Catherine standing beside and behind him, her left hand rested gently on the massive old man's equally massive left shoulder. Captain Vladov was joined by a second Soviet Special Forces officer, Lieutenant Daszrozinski, and his men.

Varakov spoke. "The assault which I propose, Dr. Rourke, is the only means by which the KGB can be prevented from fulfilling its goals. But I feel a guilt that I send you all to your deaths despite this knowledge."

I smiled and sheathed the black handled Gerber Mk II fighting knife I had added to my gear. "Captain Vladov has five men and Lieutenant Daszrozinski has five men, a total of twelve Russians, plus Natalia of course. If there were only thirteen Russians, an assault on The Womb to recover the cryogenic serum or destroy it and knock out its particle beam weapons, might be doomed to failure, I agree. But I'm an American. That'll make the difference."

I watched Natalia's eyes grow wider as I spoke. "And, if as you proposed, General Varakov, I can get the help of U.S. II in this. Two or three more Americans added to Soviet Special Forcers, will tip the scales in our favor." I added, "If mankind survives somehow after the ionization, well, history will probably show that this assault force just took advantage of those poor misguided KGB people."

Natalia began to laugh, suddenly, Captain Vladov, whom Varakov himself had labeled the best soldier in the Soviet Union, began to laugh. Lieutenant

Daszrozinski joined him, soon everyone was laughing including Varakov. His was a laugh that sounded like a child's dream of Santa Claus as it rolled sonorously from his massive body.

CHAPTER EIGHTY-TWO

Outside the Retreat the dawn had come, beautiful reds and oranges streaking across the sky. I didn't know at that time that what I should have been thinking was, *The world has not perished as it will, perhaps the next sunrise, or the next... some sunrise within the next seven days at best. All because of the electrically charged particles, the atmosphere will catch fire and spread. When it comes it will be the last sunrise for humanity.*

But, I did not know that was what I should have been thinking.

Nor did I know the only chance mankind had would be hermetically sealed shelters in Rourke's Retreat in the mountains of northeast Georgia.

We could survive the centuries while the lower plant forms gradually rebuilt the atmosphere to a level comparable to the highest altitude mountain atmospheres, but breathable. The chambers and the serum, without which the chambers would be a perpetual living death from which there could be no awakening, would allow us to awaken five centuries in the future.

Awaken to a world, however marginally, habitable. Awaken to the hoped for return of the Eden Project survivors and their microfilm libraries of the accumulated knowledge of mankind, cryogenically frozen embryonic life forms, domestic animals, livestock, even birds to sing again in the air if indeed there were air. An Ark.

But, I did not know that at the time.

Nor did I know about Colonel Nehemiah Rozhdestvenskiy, successor to Vladimir Karamatsov, the bastard husband of Major Natalia Tiemerovna, and his diabolical plan.

He would destroy the returning Eden Project before the last survivors of the world democracies could land, could reclaim the purged earth.

I also did not know that John Rourke was sitting in the semi-darkness at the height of the mezzanine steps, looking at two mastodons fight. His new mission, more than saving his wife and children, beyond saving Natalia and me and even himself for a world five centuries from now. He was to prevent the KGB Elite Corps from utilizing the cryogenic serum, destroy the particle beam weapons and prevent the ultimate Soviet domination of the entire earth, the ultimate victory for evil.

But, I did not know that at the time. I simply wondered and marveled at the bright crimson clouds and the thunder off in the distance.

CHAPTER EIGHTY-THREE

Sarah Rourke sat on one of the high rocks not far from the Retreat entrance. Her pistol, in its holster was on the ground beside her.

I sat on the next rock, an M-16 across my lap, the Schmeisser slung diagonally across my back, a Browning High Power in a shoulder holster that positioned the pistol half across the left side of my chest.

"Are you sure you're well enough?"

"It is only my left arm, Mrs. Rourke. I shoot with my right."

"I didn't mean that, and it's Sarah."

"Sarah," I nodded and pushed my wire-rimmed glasses up off the bridge of my nose with my right index finger. "Anyway, the fresh air's good for me."

She shook her head, "It is such a good feeling to have clean hair, to wash it with seemingly limitless hot water." She suddenly shivered. "What will it be like when all the supplies stored in the shelves and cabinets of John's Retreat are depleted? In the library, there are books showing how to weave cloth, books showing how to make soap from animal fat. Will we someday wear rags? Live by the light of homemade candles because the supply of light bulbs and fluorescent tubes has been depleted?"

She laughed, "What irony. Limitless electricity from the hydro electric generators John had installed, but electricity was useless without lights. I'm sorry." She grew silent.

"What is it?" I asked her.

"Nothing, I was just thinking, how stupid I'll feel someday running around in rags or animals skins cooking wild rabbit by candlelight in a microwave oven."

I started to laugh and she laughed with me. "It's nice to have something to look forward to, after all, isn't it?

CHAPTER EIGHTY-FOUR

Excerpts from an After Action Report by Colonel Reed, U.S. II, Chief of Intelligence, and conversations he had with John Rourke. <u>Colonel Reed is speaking unless otherwise indicated:</u>

I fired out my Colt 1911 and then took an M-16 from a soldier killed in the first pass the Russian helicopters had made across the school grounds. The bastards were using our own choppers against us; Huey Cobras, with a red Soviet star emblazoned over the American markings.

Over the sound of the choppers and gun fire I heard screams.

A missile hit one of the trucks at the far edge of the driveway; men and women were consumed by the fire ball. They fell from the back of the truck, their clothes and hair afire. I turned away in disgust.

When I looked back, Colonel Rubenstein was standing there. He screamed, "My wife is dead!" His hands tore at the collar of his shirt, ripping it. Suddenly, I remembered he was a Jew and I remembered that the rending of some article of clothing was a tradition for the death of a loved one.

I started to shout, "I'm sorry," but the school steps vanished..., vaporized in a ball of flame and Colonel David Rubenstein was gone.

I stabbed the M-16 skyward, firing it out uselessly, screaming the word again and again, "Bastards!" I ran toward the nearest of the trucks which could still move, shouting toward the cab, "Drive, get us out of here!"

But the truck's engine was not running. The truck beside me was hit, a shower of the material of the driveway rained down on me and flames engulfed the truck beside me; more screams and bodies on fire hurtling themselves from the vehicle. I shoved the body of the dead driver aside, cranked the truck and pumped the clutch, stomped the gas pedal, the truck started to roll forward. The gunships came in for another pass.

One of the helicopters was coming right at me; I up shifted and cranked the wheel hard left and out of the driveway. Machinegun fire blew out the window and I lost control of the truck.

The Soviet marked gunships were breaking off, disengaging. All around me... the school was awash with flames, all but two of the trucks burning or otherwise disabled. Bodies lay everywhere about the driveway, moans of the dying filling the air as the beating of the helicopter rotor blades on the air slowly began to fade.

My left hand was bleeding, my head ached badly. I staggered toward the rear of the truck, ripping back the tarpaulin cover there. The twenty or so people in the back of the truck were all dead.

I grabbed the lapel of my fatigue blouse with both hands. It was hard to tear the fabric, but on the third try... it ripped. I shouted, "For Colonel Rubenstein, for Mrs. Rubenstein... for all the dead."

CHAPTER EIGHTY-FIVE

Transcribed from a series of interviews with Natalia Anastasia Tiemerovna, Major, Committee for State Security of The Soviet. <u>Natalia speaking unless otherwise indicated:</u>

My uncle told me all of the things in the letter to John Rourke because he feared he might never see me again, and I had the right to know these things. I told him that learning about my real parents, my real mother only made me love him more.

"How goes it with the American Rourke, my child?"

"He has found his wife and children."

"What of you, child?"

"She knows, his wife knows that I love him and that he loves me. He actually loves me."

"A man does not have two wives, at least not a man like this Dr. John Rourke. Perhaps he thinks of the Jew, Rubenstein, of him for you should the Eden Project not return."

"I told Paul that I loved him, but that I love him like my brother, and I would rather go on loving John Rourke and have him never touch me than to lie that I could love someone else." We talked awhile longer, he trying to understand my feelings.

My uncle said something so sweet, "Your heart, it has always been the heart of your real mother. Did I tell you in the letter that her name was Natalia?"

I nodded.

"An old man forgets, child. But there are some things... some things that an old man can never..." He ceased to speak.

"Forget," I whispered for him.

He nodded and said, "There are some things, and perhaps for you, John Rourke is such a thing. Would that your mother had so worshiped me as evident as you worship this Rourke. If you love him so, then respect him also for what he is and what he is not and would never pretend to be."

*****

My Reflection:

Those words have followed me all of these years... Love is a many splendored thing... but it will tear your guts out.

CHAPTER EIGHTY-SIX

Transcribed from a series of interviews with John Rourke. <u>John Rourke is speaking unless otherwise indicated:</u>

Varakov told me to be clear of the museum by eight forty-five at the latest and it was almost eight-thirty. But rushing Natalia's last farewell to her uncle was something I couldn't do.

I had removed my pack for the third time, placing it on one of the benches at the rear of the mezzanine, my M-16 beside it, only the CAR-15 slung cross body from my left shoulder when I heard footsteps. Natalia was walking slowly beside her uncle. I signaled Vladov's man and turned to speak to Vladov himself.

I asked him how he felt about going against other Russians like himself at The Womb? He said simply they were other Russians, but "they are not like myself."

"Fair enough," I said and turned back to Natalia. Varakov, beside her, stopped as he reached the edge of the mezzanine.

"General Varakov, I think we could have been friends if all of us hadn't been so bent on butchering each other, Sir," I said.

"I think that you are quite correct, Dr. Rourke. You will care for her... I trust you and you alone with the greatest joy of my life."

"I know that, Sir." Our hands were still clasped.

"We communists are taught that there is no God to believe in... but in the event we have been wrong all these decades since we attempted to liberate man from his chains, then I wish that, God, if He exists, will bless you all and protect you."

I smiled, "We capitalists are taught that hedging your bet is never a bad thing, General. May God bless you, too."

The old man nodded, his eyes lit with something I could not read, but something somehow I understood.

Varakov folded Natalia into his arms, speaking to her in Russian. "I love you, you are the daughter, you are the life I never led. Kiss me goodbye, child... forever."

She did and came to stand beside me. Behind me, Captain Vladov and Lieutenant Daszrozinski stood at stiff attention, right hands raised in salute.

As I looked back to Varakov, the old man, his uniform tunic open, his shoes unlaced, his shirt collar open, returned the salute sharply. "God, if He hears me and if He is there to begin with, God speed."

CHAPTER EIGHTY-SEVEN

Transcribed from a series of interviews with John Rourke continued. <u>John Rourke is speaking unless otherwise indicated:</u>

I looked back, once. Varakov, his secretary Catherine, beside him, stood at the balcony of the mezzanine, only staring. "Let's go," I said. "Our best tribute to him is to do what the General called us here for, Captain."

"Agreed."

"Natalia?"

Her blue eyes awash with tears, she nodded. "Yes."

*****

The sun was higher over the lake than I would have thought, thunder rumbled in the sky to the east as we raced down the museum steps toward the lanes of Lake Shore Drive. The click of the Soviet Special Forces troopers' boots on the stone steps was loud and oddly reassuring.

My Rolex said it was eight forty-two. At eight forty-five, for some reason Varakov had specified, there could be trouble. Behind me Vladov said, "Look there, Dr. Rourke from the south! KGB!" We ran, but by the time we got to the low sea wall... we were trapped.

"What do we do, Comrade Major?" Vladov asked, sounding slightly out of breath. "Do we wait here or proceed?"

"Those trucks," Natalia panted. "They are heading for Meigg's Field?"

"Yes, Comrade Major. Each day the KGB has been shipping out supplies by nine-fifteen. We do not know what."

"How big are the planes they use?" I asked.

"They are American Boeing KC-135Bs."

I nodded. "There were steel mills beyond the bend in the shoreline, could be billets of steel. Maybe Rozhdestvenskiy wants some laid in at The Womb to handle early construction after the awakening."

"My uncle has the boats waiting just beyond the planetarium. Some of the GRU men he trusted are with them, but they are not insane. If we wait and do not make our rendezvous they will leave and we will be stranded here."

CHAPTER EIGHTY-EIGHT

Transcribed from historical artifacts of the government of U.S. II located in an archaeological dig, in area formerly identified as Texas:

Sam Chambers, president of U.S. II: "This is butchery, pure butchery!"

Colonel Reed: "It proves what I've been saying, Mr. President, a major Soviet offensive directed against us. They're softening us up. That's why they did this. Demoralize us. For the last two weeks at least, there've been all the signs. Airborne reconnaissance shows units of the Army and KGB units too, massing in east Texas and in central Louisiana. They're going to hit us right between 'em."

Chambers: "Your efforts to contact the reorganized Texas volunteer militia?"

Reed: "I don't know, Sir. I sent Lieutenant Feltcher out three weeks ago, haven't heard from him since. We just don't know, Sir."

Chambers: "But they're the only hope we have."

Reed: "If they come and link up with us before the Russians strike, then we can beat this Russian force. If they get caught up with the Russians in east Texas, then we can take on the Russians in central Louisiana. If they don't come at all, it's either surrender or be crushed. It'd be a slaughter."

Chambers: "We won't surrender."

Reed: "I didn't think we would, Sir."

CHAPTER EIGHTY-NINE

Transcribed from a series of interviews with John Rourke, continued.
<u>**John Rourke is speaking unless otherwise indicated:**</u>

We reached land's end where three six-man Avon rubber boats, the kind divers sometimes use, waited for us with a solitary man standing by each boat holding an AK-47; standing guard.

Natalia murmured, "GRU." She stood up, the rocks shielding her from view further back along the land. She stepped from behind the rocks, her voice a low whisper, "I am Major Tiemerovna, gentlemen. You wait for me?" The guard nodded. "You are ready for our departure?" she asked.

"Yes, Comrade Major, but the outboard engines, they are loud. If the KGB should hear they could open fire at us, these are only rubber boats and not bullet resistant."

A KGB patrol was right behind us. We were trapped, we would have to fight our way out and Natalia wanted to fight... so I gave her a quick clip to the chin, knocking her out. Captain Vladov and I would stay behind with one other man and take out those KGB patrolmen. One of the GRU men would have to stay behind to keep the boat ready and signal the other two boats to start their engines and make time.

"I will stay," a GRU man volunteered.

"Good," Daszrozinski and two other men had already climbed down from the rocks into the nearest of the Avon rubber boats; I put Natalia into Daszrozinski's and a second man's arms. "When the major wakes up, well, tell her not to be mad at me, huh?"

Daszrozinski's very Slavic, red-cheeked face showed a grin. "I will try my best, Dr. Rourke."

Chapter Ninety

Transcribed from a series of interviews with Natalia Tiemerovna. <u>Natalia is speaking unless otherwise indicated:</u>

When I woke up, Lieutenant Daszrozinski told me that John, Captain Vladov and one other man were seeing to the KGB patrol. One of the GRU men was waiting with the third boat. He would signal when we can start our engines.

I realized that at any minute, the occupants of the police car would look out onto the lake and see our boats and they would start shooting. This far off shore, our marksmanship would have little effect. Maximum effective range of the AKM—what the KGB patrols were armed with—was three hundred meters on full auto, four hundred meters semi-automatic mode, if the shooter was an exceptional marksmen. If they were, they would have been assigned other duties so, logically, I was in no danger.

But John was much closer than four hundred meters, or three hundred meters. He could very easily be killed by even an indifferent marksman.

CHAPTER NINETY-ONE

Transcribed from a series of interviews with John Rourke. <u>John Rourke is speaking unless otherwise indicated:</u>

I raced along the rocks of the sea wall and positioned myself on the far side of the planetarium, behind the police car, and waited.

The three KGB patrolmen exited the police car, two carrying assault rifles, but all three wearing pistols in military flap holsters on their belts. I left the M-16 and the CAR-15 behind with Vladov and Corporal Ravitski, the long bladed Gerber Mk II in my right fist as I followed the men. Ravitski's job was the most unpleasant, to take out the man who regularly urinated over the side of the sea wall.

For the purpose, he had long handled wire cutters he had taken from the side of his backpack, Vladov backed him up. The man trying to empty his kidneys took two steps forward, toward the sea wall, the other two men, the one still laughing, turned their backs as he bent forward.

Suddenly, the body sagged forward. Ravitski's long handled wire cutters had done their grisly work, snipping off the man's penis.

The two men turned back, reaching out, groping toward the sea wall to snatch at the body of their stricken comrade. At a dead run, I leaped airborne, and threw myself forward, the Gerber reaching out, the spear pointed tip thrusting into the back of the man to his right, severing the spinal cord.

The second man starting to turn, my left hand punched forward, the point of the little Sting 1A black chrome puncturing the Adam's apple, cutting through, the man's eyes wide open, no voice box left with which to scream.

Vladov came up from the sea wall beyond, his fighting knife, a bastardized Bowie pattern, hacking left to right across the throat of the man I had stabbed with the big Gerber, severing the carotid artery and slicing through the voice box before there could be a scream.

My right hand thrust upward, palm open into the nose of the man with the little A.G. Russell knife in his throat, punching the bone upward, through the ethmoid bone and into the brain. My left hand ripping the knife downward through the Adam's apple and locking against the bone beneath the hollow of the throat.

"Let's get the hell out of here, have the GRU man give the signal." I heard the drone of the outboard motors already started up. I heard aircraft engines revving, from the field, and realized, there was no sound of police sirens... not yet.

Chapter Ninety-Two

**Transcribed from a series of interviews with John Rourke, continued.
<u>John Rourke is speaking unless otherwise indicated:</u>**

We ditched the rubber boats and transferred to a medium sized cabin cruis-
er and went out farther into the lake. It was late afternoon by the time we
pulled ashore near Waukegan where abandoned factory complexes littered the
shoreline.

We worked our way to the rear door of the American field hospital which
was in reality Resistance headquarters for the area and made contact with Tom
Maus.

I told Maus there was one last mission, to maybe save some of humanity
and that we needed his help. Maus wasn't happy about our KGB and GRU
friends but agreed to a meet if, "Some of my people keep their guns drawn."

Natalia said, "Fine, but don't mind if some of my people keep their guns
drawn, too."

"I need your help making contact with U.S. II on the radio," I told the Resistance leader. Fear of the radio being tracked down created resistance but in
the end a transmission was made. It took two tries and an authentication code
to get through but we did. I told them to get a message to President Chambers
that John Rourke said in six days the world was going to end.

CHAPTER NINETY-THREE

Transcribed from artifacts located in an archaeological dig, in an area formerly identified as the Museum of Natural History, Chicago:

Contact was finally made with President Samuel Chambers. He was glad to hear that the Eden Project had in fact gotten away in time before the Kennedy Space Center was destroyed.

Chambers: "I cannot send you a large force, Dr. Rourke. I can send you a dozen volunteers. No others can be spared. KGB forces and Army units under KGB command have our backs to the wall here, boxing us in. Our only chance is volunteers from Texas. Colonel Reed has told me I'm stupid to be saying this without it being in code, but what's the difference now.

"I should have known a set up for a slaughter like this wasn't General Varakov's doing. They've been making strafing runs on hospitals, bombing civilian encampments, the whole thing. The largest troop commitment they've made since invading the continent. I've got you a volunteer, your old friend Colonel Reed. Where do I send him and the men he'll take with him?"

Rourke: "I saw Reed with a western novel once. I recall reading the author was particularly interested in a certain location. For four reasons. See if he understands, Rourke over."

Reed: Half laughing said, "Rourke, I'd love to meet you there, love it."

Rourke: "Get there as quick as you can and bring everything you can carry."

CHAPTER NINETY-FOUR

Excerpts from an After Action Report by Colonel Reed, U.S. II, Chief of Intelligence. <u>Colonel Reed speaking unless otherwise indicated:</u>

My volunteers had been told they were volunteering for what was likely a suicide mission. Apparently the Russians were going to destroy what was called the Eden Project.

In six days at the most, perhaps at dawn tomorrow, the sky would catch fire. The atmosphere would all but completely burn away and the earth itself will burn. We would all die then anyway. But apparently the Russians had some system for surviving it somewhere.

I suspect we were going to old NORAD Headquarters at Cheyenne Mountain but we won't know that until we rendezvous with Rourke and his force. It's our job to knock out the Russian base, so they can't survive the holocaust.

Otherwise, when the people of the Eden Project return to earth, the KGB would be waiting for them, to shoot down the space shuttles before they land. And the Russians will have won it all; Communism will have the ultimate triumph.

I told my people that we owed it to the future, if there is one, and to every man and woman alive today or whoever lived, whoever sacrificed life or security or pleasure to defend the ideal of freedom, we owed it to all of them not to let Communism win, not to let the KGB be the masters of earth.

And dying fighting for that is a hell of a lot better than being incinerated when the end comes. Then I was sorry I had said "hell," remembering suddenly I was standing in a church.

One of the men asked what good could twelve of us do against the might of the Soviet Union? I told the men it was not just twelve, Rourke had some volunteers, I didn't know. Maybe a Resistance group or something. Maybe there would be a couple dozen of us.

And what could we do?

Everything.

Anything.

Die, if that's the only way. But we would do what we could. I told them I didn't want a single man with me who isn't ready to give it his best shot. Maybe we had the chance here to eradicate all the pent-up evil in the world all at once, to give mankind a fresh start five hundred years from now. And... maybe we don't.

But as Americans, well, we gotta try it.

I looked at my Timex and told the men we should be moving out, but any man who wanted not to go, well stay in the church here a while and pray for those of us who do. I won't think any the less of him.

One of the men stood and said, "I think we all wanna go, Sir. But could you maybe lead us in a moment's prayer, Sir?"

I told him I'd rather he did it as I wasn't too experienced at praying.

"Colonel, Sir," he said, "I think the men'd rather that you did, Sir."

I nodded, closed my eyes and bowed my head. "Heavenly Father, help us to see your will and to do it. And bless us all for trying. Amen." I told the Sergeant, "See, I said I was an amateur at it."

"It sounded pretty good to me, Colonel."

We started down the aisle of the church, when the strangest thing happened; a young corporal began singing, "Onward Christian soldiers..."

The sergeant's voice joined him, "Marching as to war..."

I didn't know the words perfectly, and I felt almost silly. My wife always joked I couldn't carry a tune with both hands and a bucket. But I joined my men anyway. "... leads against the foe; Forward into battle, see his banners go."

I am leaving this report here for safe keeping. Should someone make it through all of this, should someday someone read these words... I don't know. Maybe it will fill in some blanks for history.

Maybe someone that has not even been born yet will learn about how we died.

Maybe someone will remember...

CHAPTER NINETY-FIVE

Transcribed from a series of interviews with John Rourke. <u>John Rourke is speaking unless otherwise indicated:</u>

After the call to President Chambers and my cryptic message to Reed, Natalia had looked confused, I told her that I was talking about the most famous western writer in history. His name in French meant love and he was fascinated by "The Four Corners."

She smiled. "Louis L'Amour, and where Utah, Colorado, Arizona and New Mexico's state boundaries all meet."

"Yup."

*****

We walked in darkness, the airfield Varakov had arranged for the GRU pick up was still perhaps a quarter mile away. Tom Maus said, "I've been thinking pretty hard about this. I haven't mentioned it to any of the others yet, but I'm planning on starting an all out offensive against the Russians in metropolitan Chicago."

"Go down fighting?" I asked.

"Something like that, but more than that. Ever since the Russians moved in, they've been using Soldiers' Field Stadium as an internment camp and their medical headquarters. They have other internment camps there; they treat the prisoners well enough. But it's the idea, the people there aren't free. Americans shouldn't die that way if they have to die. Penned up, under guard. Maybe it is that, go down fighting. They should have that chance, the Americans the Communists are holding."

"I'll ask a favor," I said seriously. "Don't make a direct assault on Soviet Headquarters at the museum. Let Varakov die his own way."

"Agreed," Maus answered. "That's the funny thing, the way Major Tiemerovna spoke about her uncle, before and in the truck just now, and what he's done now to fight the KGB, General Varakov sounds like a good man."

One of the men said, "Kind of stupid, isn't it, I mean, if you assume we're good men, too. Why were we fighting each other all these years?" I didn't have an answer for him.

CHAPTER NINETY-SIX

Transcribed from a series of interviews with John Rourke, continued.
John Rourke is speaking unless otherwise indicated:

The GRU aircraft, a Beechcraft Super King Air, made its pass over the field. Vladov radioed the aircraft, getting the proper recognition signal. There had been a schedule of appointed rendezvous times, five in all and this was the fourth. The Beechcraft touched down, bouncing across the field, slowing, slowing still more, then turning into a takeoff position.

I felt like a drug dealer waiting for a marijuana drop. Natalia, Maus, Vladov and a guy named Stanonik were in a wedge around me. It was a two-hundred yard run with a heavy pack. The door in the fuselage opened, a tall, thin man appearing in the shadow and moonlight. He looked down. "You are the American doctor?"

"I'm Rourke."

I felt Natalia's presence beside me. "I know you, you are Captain Gorki. I met you once in Moscow."

"You remember faces well. I am Major Gorki now. It is good to see you, Comrade."

Tom Maus came up from the nose of the plane, dipping under the starboard wing. "You'd better get airborne and get the hell out of here."

Vladov and Daszrozinski, Daszrozinski leading the Soviet SFers toward the fuselage. I stepped away to give them room. The GRU pilot had hopped down. "Dr. Rourke, there are two of us, myself and a Sergeant Druszik. We will accompany you, Comrade Major Tiemerovna, and be ready to fly you out should that be possible.

"I couldn't inform U.S. II of the exact rendezvous point we'd been given, the possibility of the KGB listening in was too great. But I'll give you a new rendezvous spot, easy enough to get to."

****

I sat in the shelter of high rocks, overlooking the only logical landing site for an aircraft of sufficient size to land a dozen men and a crew. Natalia slept in my left arm, her head against my shoulder. Only Vladov, and two other men were awake.

I looked at Tom Maus. "Tom, if I don't get the chance later... good luck to you."

"And to you."

Vladov said, "This Colonel Reed of whom you speak. What is he like? I have heard of him before. The chief intelligence officer for United States II."

I smiled. "He is that. Strange guy, fluctuates from an occasionally bizarre sense of humor to a guy who wouldn't laugh if his life depended on it. He's a career man, Army Intelligence on active duty for a long time, then in the Reserves, then called up to active duty when all of this started, before the War."

"He hates Russians then."

"Yeah, he hates Russians with a real passion."

"It is something very strange," Vladov said. "But before The Night of The War, I hated Americans very much. And I realized after our troops came in as part of the first invasion force, I had never met an American. Not ever. I wondered how it could be that I could hate someone whom I had never come to know. I still wonder this."

"You'll turn into a pacifist if you're not careful," I laughed softly.

"Yes, a pacifist. It would be most amusing for me to turn into a pacifist. I fought in Afghanistan. I served in a security contingent in Poland. It should be most amusing were I to become a pacifist, as you say."

"I was pretty much the same way. I met Natalia, saved her life, and she saved mine, mine and my friend Paul Rubenstein..."

"This Rubenstein is Jewish, correct?"

"Yeah," I nodded, not mentioning that Natalia was also half Jewish as her uncle had revealed in his letter.

"In Russia, we do not like Jews."

"You ever think maybe all of that was just as smart as not liking Americans?"

The Soviet Special Forces captain didn't answer for a moment, then from the sudden darkness when a cloud blocked the moon, Rourke heard his voice. "You do not hate the Russians?"

"I don't hate her, do I? And I can't see any reason to hate you. Do you hate me?"

"No, of course not, there is..."

"No reason?"

"Yes, no reason."

"Too bad," I smiled. "Too bad we couldn't have all sat down like this before it all got blown up and destroyed, before this whole holocaust scenario came about."

"Too bad, yes. This Eden Project, perhaps for them it will be different. If we can do what we have set out here to do."

"Perhaps," I agreed. "But in a way, maybe it won't be."

"What do you mean?" Vladov asked, the flare of a match cupped in his hands.

"It'd be nice if somehow they could know what we're talking of here tonight, and learn from our mistakes. It'd be nice if they could."

"Yes."

"But I don't think they will, you got an extra cigarette? If I light a cigar, the smell will wake up Natalia."

"I hope you like them," I heard Vladov laugh. "They are American cigarettes."

"Any port in a storm."

Vladov fired the cigarette from his own already lit one, passed it to me. In the distance, I heard the drone of aircraft engines. I turned my body to read my watch. It was set still to Eastern time. In an hour or so, in the East, it would be sunrise. It was hard to think that in Europe, in what remained of Great Britain, perhaps the world had already ended.

I inhaled the cigarette smoke deeply into my lungs, wondering what it mattered. But I felt Natalia's breath against my skin as she moved and realized that it still did matter.

CHAPTER NINETY-SEVEN

Transcribed from a series of interviews with John Rourke, continued.
John Rourke is speaking unless otherwise indicated:

Vladov aroused his men and they went out onto the prairie, lighting the flares already set there after their arrival. There were no radio communications, to have agreed on a frequency would have been risking the security compromised.

The aircraft, an old civilian aircraft I couldn't immediately identify, slowed, turning, prepared for takeoff. The fuselage door opened, men poured from it, dropping flat in the high grass.

I woke Natalia and along with Vladov, walked across the prairie, the grass high, nearly to my knees in spots. I saw Reed standing beside the wing stem.

"I should have figured you'd have her with you, Rourke."

Natalia answered. "I too looked forward to seeing you again, Colonel Reed."

"That's not Rubenstein unless he's grown a couple of inches; got yourself a new sidekick, have you?"

"I found Sarah and the children. Paul was injured. He's recovering at the Retreat and looking after my family."

"Good for you, you should spend these last few days with them, why the hell are you here?"

"A job to do." I stopped walking, standing two yards or so from Reed. I had seen the bristling of Reed's men when they had spotted Vladov's Soviet fatigue uniform.

"That's a clever disguise; he looks just like a Russian Special Forces captain."

"Colonel Reed, I am Captain Vladov, at your service, Sir." Vladov saluted. I watched this from the corner of my right eye. Reed didn't move. Vladov held the salute.

"I'm not in full uniform, Captain," Reed nodded, gesturing to his hatless condition. Vladov held the salute.

Reed snapped, "Shit," then returned the salute.

A smile etched across my lips. "Glad to see you haven't mellowed, Reed."

"You got any more Russians, or just these two?"

Natalia answered. "There are eleven other Soviet Special Forces personnel, surrounding the field."

I wanted to laugh, she couldn't pass it up. "One officer and ten enlisted personnel. In addition, one officer and one enlisted from GRU."

"Aww, that's fuckin' wonderful. What we got here, a Commie convention?"

"What we've got," I answered, "is fourteen highly skilled men who value human decency over dialectics. You got any problems with that, climb back on your goddamn airplane and we'll knock out The Womb all by ourselves."

There was some haggling but in the end, Reed bent a little and we had a cohesive team. Or at least the beginnings of one. While a white-haired master sergeant named Dressler barked orders to help Vladov remove the camouflage for the airplane, I watched Reed. He said, "By the way, if I don't get the chance, tell Rubenstein, I was with his mother and father when they died." His voice did something I had never seen with Reed, it quivered. "Tell him they sent their love and were together at the end. Will ya do that for me?"

I nodded.

CHAPTER NINETY-EIGHT

Transcribed from a series of interviews with John Rourke, continued.
<u>John Rourke is speaking unless otherwise indicated:</u>

The two planes had dropped us about ten miles from the main entrance of the Cheyenne Mountain underground complex. The light around it was grey as we walked. In another mile or so, I would send out an advance party to scout for Soviet patrols. I was holding back.

In a few moments we would reach the height of the lower elevation peak and from there, be able to see the horizon. If it were aflame, sending out an advance party would be pointless. We would all be dead in minutes.

I looked at Natalia, "If it happens, I shall love you after death as well." Then I realized that if this morning was THE morning and that if my wife and children and Paul... if they had been caught outside, or failed to completely secure the Retreat... they were dead.

We topped the last rise, the sun, lightning crackled round it in the air on the horizon, but there were no flames.

Natalia smiled. "There is another day, John."

"Yes."

Chapter Ninety-Nine

Transcribed directly from reports of <u>Nehemiah Rozhdestvenskiy</u>, Commander of the North American Branch of The Committee for State Security of the Soviet and discovered at an archaeological dig at the former Cheyenne Mountain complex:

Report # 67204, Personal: I watched as the master radar control screen depicted the blips. The Corpsman monitoring the screens declared them to be an Aeroflot passenger jet and six Mikoyan/Gurevich MiG-27 fighters ninety miles out.

I ordered the system be energized to ready status. When the planes were sixty-five miles out I directed a Sergeant to order the airfield prepared for reception of the premier, the Politburo and the Committee Leadership.

I told the Duty Officer to begin tracking. My aide said the system had been energized to ready status. The high resolution television monitors overhead in the command center had only faint images and I told the technician to get greater resolution. The image suddenly changed on the screen and I could see them. One large, passenger sized aircraft and six smaller aircraft, the fighters. The Duty Officer confirmed he was tracking them. I picked up the microphone to the Firing Center and gave final instructions and began the countdown. I ordered the laser charge through the particle chamber activated.

I had memorized the firing sequences, learned the very functioning of the system itself to be sure. I could trust it to no one else's hands; I was both the commander and technician. I increased power from one-quarter to full power and boosted ionization fifteen points. I ordered the technician to hold capacitance to ten to the seventeenth capacitance with zero flux.

Over the radar screen, a grid of green lines appeared, the Theta grid appeared on Camera 1; it matched the lines on the radar screen. I designated the targets, licked my lips and ordered, "Automatic target acquisition and destruction on my mark... six, five, four, three, two, one. Mark!"

One instant, the Aeroflot aircraft carrying the Politburo, the premier, the leaders of the KGB, was there. Then there was a blinding flash of light and when I opened my eyes seventeen seconds later, the airline was gone.

Then the camera totally malfunctioned and we lost video. I laughed, I realized all of them thought I was suddenly insane but the master of an entire planet could afford the luxury.

Signed

<original signed>

Nehemiah Rozhdestvenskiy, Colonel. Commander of the North American Branch of The Committee for State Security of the Soviet.

CHAPTER ONE HUNDRED

Transcribed from a series of interviews with John Rourke. <u>John Rourke is speaking unless otherwise indicated:</u>

"Holy shit, what the hell was that. Has it started?" Reed shouted looking at the sky.

There was fire in the sky, a pencil-thin beam of light visible for an instant. I shouted, "Look away!" and grabbed Natalia and pulled her to the ground; the roar from above, deafening now.

The roar gradually died and I opened my eyes, Natalia's blue eyes staring at me.

"Was that it?" Reed snarled. "But we're still alive..."

"That wasn't the ionization," I said. "It was the particle beam system."

"My uncle had predicted Rozhdestvenskiy would do this thing," Natalia said. "And he was right. He has just destroyed the entire Soviet government. He has killed them all. He has made himself... he has made himself the master of the entire world, should we fail."

It was one of the U.S. II troopers who spoke, one of the two black men of the group. "Me, ma'am, don't like folks what thinks they're somebody else's master. We're gonna have to get that sucker. Get him good, we are."

I helped Natalia to stand, her hands were shaking. "The corporal said it, we're gonna have to get Rozhdestvenskiy, gonna have to get him good. Reed, you and Vladov pick some men, ones who can be good and quiet. Put out a recon element so we don't go walking into something."

"I'll take 'em, Sir," Sergeant Dressler said, pulling his fatigue cap off, running his five pound ham-sized right hand through his hair then replacing the cap.

"All right, Sergeant, co-ordinate with Captain Vladov," Reed nodded.

"I think," Vladov said quietly, "that the good Colonel Rozhdestvenskiy has just made all of us into one unit, has he not?"

CHAPTER ONE HUNDRED ONE

Transcribed from a series of interviews with John Rourke, continued.
John Rourke is speaking unless otherwise indicated:

With my armored Bushnell 8x30s , I peered across the corridors of granite at the entrance of Cheyenne Mountain. A level plain was before it, when I had seen the complex once years ago, there had been a single twelve foot high chain link fence with electrified barbed wire at the top. Now, perhaps twenty yards forward of this, there was a second fence of identical seeming construction.

Men armed with M-16s traveled the area between the fence in pairs, one of each pair restraining a guard dog on a leash, the dogs either Dobermans or German Shepherds. The sentries were at three minute intervals, hardly enough time to cross the outer perimeter electrified fence and reach the inner fence, let alone cross it.

First problem... breaking into The Womb. The second would be stealing the chambers, the serum and the third would be breaking back out.

Natalia had been given detailed information gathered by the GRU detailing Womb defenses. Including the fact that in addition to the human and canine sentries, the area between the two fences was covered with closed circuit television cameras with at least four operators manning the camera monitors at all times.

Beyond the interior fence for a distance of twenty yards was a mine field, the nature of the mines... unknown. A smaller fence, perhaps eight feet high, formed the third and innermost boundary.

Running through the boundaries was one road, two lanes wide at best; it passed through the gates and toward the base of the mountain. Forming an outside perimeter some five yards or so before reaching the first twelve foot electrified fence were concrete barriers.

Flanking the main entrance were two 155mm M 198 Howitzer guns. The exterior bombproof doors were fabricated of a special titanium alloy, given special heat treatment and constructed of various layers.

Inside, a similar single door, twice the thickness, weighing literally tons, was positioned. This massive vault door was rigged to a combination lock system and automatically closed and hermetically sealed the complex when the facility went to final alert status and unable to be opened until the alert status was cancelled in a specified manner.

To the south, lay the airfield which served the mountain. A central section of the main runway functioned like the elevators aboard an aircraft carrier, able to raise or lower planes to or from the runway surface. A similar system of fences, guards and blast barriers formed a perimeter surrounding the field, although GRU doubted the area between the second and third smaller fence would be mined, this in the event of a landing or takeoff difficulty.

Teams of sentries utilizing guard dogs roamed the field in seemingly random patterns. As an aircraft would make an approach, the sentries would disperse, then claxons would sound again and the sentries would resume their random seeming patterns of movement across the field.

Once the elevator would lower an aircraft to the below ground hangar complex, there was a system of doors duplicating exactly the main door system. In addition, the runway elevator had sliding panels which could be brought into place to bombproof this opening as well.

At the height of the mountain, in what appeared almost a dish shaped valley, but the dish of concrete, looking for all the world like a massive radio telescope, were the particle beam weapons. These were ringed by conventional radar controlled anti-aircraft guns and banks of surface to air missiles.

The particle beam devices rose perhaps five hundred feet skyward on huge crane-like gantries. There were two of these and the mountings at their bases seemed mobile which would give each unit more than one hundred eighty degrees of movement and nearly a full one hundred eighty degrees of movement from the horizontal. A low flying aircraft could get under their range of movement but the surface to air missiles and anti-aircraft guns would take care of that possibility.

Natalia whispered from beside me. "It is impregnable, The Womb, isn't it?"

"... As impregnable as anything can be made. We can't sneak in, we can't shoot our way in, we can't blast our way in with explosives, we can't fly in, we can't rappel down into it. We can't even wait until nightfall—the infrared system the GRU said they have, the starlight systems.

"And anyway, the main doors are closed and The Womb is hermetically sealed in the event of the next dawn bringing the ionization effect. We can't even crash a plane into the particle beam weapons. A plane big enough to carry sufficient explosives wouldn't fly low enough to avoid the system, and even if the system were down and they didn't have time to bring it up to emit the pulse, the antiaircraft guns and the surface to air missiles would knock us out.

"Maybe a thousand planes, all of the pilots kamikazes, each aircraft carrying a nuclear weapon... maybe that'd do some good. And besides, even if we knocked out the particle beam weapons so Rozhdestvenskiy couldn't use them against the Eden Project when it returns, he'd have time to rebuild them, possibly once it was safe to move about on the surface again.

"If we don't destroy their cryogenics ability, a thousand highly trained men from the KGB Elite Corps would be more than a match for one hundred and thirty-eight men and women who are scientists, doctors, teachers, pilots, farmers, like that."

"It is impossible," Natalia whispered, her eyes wide, staring at what I didn't know.

I smiled, "But that's to our advantage. Making it impossible for us will force us to try something thoroughly desperate, something only people who were doomed and had no alternatives would try. And that's the sort of thing no system of security can be made to anticipate."

"Then we have a chance?"

"If there's one thing I believe in, besides you, besides Sarah and the children, besides Paul's friendship, I believe that as long as you never give up, you've always got a chance. So yeah, we have a chance."

I shifted the binoculars back to my eyes, watching the entrance to The Womb. Just what exactly our chances might be, of that I wasn't certain.

CHAPTER ONE HUNDRED TWO

Transcribed directly from a report by <u>Nehemiah Rozhdestvenskiy</u>, Commander of the North American Branch of The Committee for State Security of the Soviet and discovered at an archaeological dig at the former Cheyenne Mountain complex:

Report # 67205, Personal: I have to admit to a certain letdown. I sit quietly in my office, smoking a cigarette, studying my Colt Single Action Army revolver which lay on the desk beside me. I will never need to use it again. There are no more enemies to fight.

I rule the world. It had been the dream of Caesar, of Alexander, of Napoleon, of Hitler, perhaps of Stalin. But I have achieved it.

In seventy years after the awakening, my population could easily triple. It is believed that the cryogenic process serves to restore the body while it sleeps. If that is the case, perhaps...

My parents and grandparents were long lived. Perhaps, my life span may surpass theirs. Disease on the new earth will be virtually unknown, the same process which will destroy all sentient life will destroy most if not all of the world's disease producing organisms. A world without infectious disease. A Garden of Eden, and I shall be its master. A barren garden at first, but the plants, the embryonic animals which were even now being cryogenically frozen under the aegis of that fool, Professor Zlovski. Damn his eyes.

I have stared at myself in the mirror on the wall of this office and have seen the face of God, my own face.

Signed

<original signed>

Nehemiah Rozhdestvenskiy, Colonel. Commander of the North American Branch of The Committee for State Security of the Soviet.

CHAPTER ONE HUNDRED THREE

Transcribed from a series of interviews with John Rourke. <u>John Rourke is speaking unless otherwise indicated:</u>

The roadway leading down from Cheyenne Mountain, was patrolled by four wheel drive vehicles, each with one driver and two guards, each vehicle fitted with an RPK 7.62mm light machinegun and a seventy-five round drum magazine.

Natalia, Reed, Vladov and I watched the road from a quarter mile distant. Reed said, "If all these people speak Russian like natives..."

"We are natives, Colonel," Vladov interjected.

"Anyway," Reed observed, "we might be able to bluff our way through if we can take over one of the smaller convoys. But how the hell we're gonna do that with those patrols on the road I don't know."

Natalia began, taking a cigarette; I lit it for her with my Zippo. "We were taught that what is familiar is the least suspected. We can utilize this to our advantage. We have, after all, twelve men in Soviet uniform who are in fact Soviet soldiers."

I smiled, "I think what Natalia's getting at is that those guys in the road patrols can't be too high up the echelon. What if Captain Vladov and Lieutenant Daszrozinski marched their men down onto the roadway and flagged down one of the patrol vehicles, then take out the guys running it."

"And then," Natalia smiled, "the captain could replace the three soldiers with three of his own men. It would merely involve changing uniform blouses. The vehicle proceeds down the highway toward a convoy of sufficiently small size which we have pre-selected and stops the convoy. If another of the patrols comes by, it can be waved off. The suspicions of the convoy would not be aroused, there are so many of the road patrols that they must by now be a familiar sight to them."

"Maybe the Jeep could be given a flat tire or something and stopping the convoy would seem more natural," Reed said.

"Exactly," Natalia nodded. "And once the convoy is stopped, the rest of us sweep down to attack."

"We eliminate the personnel of the convoy," Vladov said, as if thinking out loud. "Assuming they are KGB, we take their uniforms."

We agreed that knives would be better than guns if we could get away with it. If the knife work is done properly, there can be little bleeding to stain the uniform. We get the convoy orders, drive up there and fake it.

Reed nodded. "Why don't I send some of my guys down the road where it bends there to find a likely convoy. I'll space men a half mile apart and use them as relay runners to get the information back here."

"Good, we can't risk radio here. Don't know what frequency the convoys use, or what frequency the patrols use." I turned to Natalia. "You go with Reed's men, run the thing, unless you have some objections, Colonel Reed."

"Naw, I wanna get the job done, however we do it, I can object later, if there is a later."

"Agreed," Natalia nodded.

I turned to Captain Vladov. "I saw one of your men with a 7.62 SVD with a PS0-1 telescopic sight; have him leave that with me so I can long distance any trouble you might have if I need to. I left my SSG at the Retreat."

"Of course, Doctor."

"We all set then?"

Reed said to Vladov, "Good luck, I mean with nailing that patrol vehicle, Captain."

"Thank you, Colonel."

Natalia smiled.

CHAPTER ONE HUNDRED FOUR

Transcribed from a series of interviews with John Rourke, continued.
<u>John Rourke is speaking unless otherwise indicated:</u>

Reed had stayed behind in the rocks with me. The veteran, white-haired Sergeant Dressler, accompanied Natalia and the American force. They moved along a ridge line at a brisk, stiff-legged, long stride Commando walk. Dressler seemed to show no fatigue.

Natalia told him she had studied at the Polytechnic and was qualified as an engineer of sorts in electronics and had studied ballet. Dressler told her, "I bet you was pretty as a ballerina, Major. Ma'am, you think we got a prayer of gettin' in there and doin' what we gotta do?"

"A prayer, Sergeant, I should think we have that at least."

CHAPTER ONE HUNDRED FIVE

Transcribed from a series of interviews with John Rourke, continued.
<u>John Rourke is speaking unless otherwise indicated:</u>

I watched Captain Vladov through the sniper scope walking briskly along the trail leading down from the rocks. Lieutenant Daszrozinski was beside him, the ten other Special Forces troopers behind and walking two abreast.

He had intentionally taken no security precautions, friendly forces in friendly territory needed no such precautions and to bring off the ruse, openness, innocence; these were necessary, more crucial than guile.

He withdrew the Walther pistol Natalia had loaned him from beneath his tunic, edged the slide slightly rearward, re-checking that a round was chambered. He gave the silencer a firm twist, but it was already locked firmly in place.

His first target would be the machine gunner at the back of the vehicle. If his men had not dispatched the driver and the second man by the time he had killed the machine gunner, he would turn the pistol on them.

*****

I saw the sentry vehicle and fed a 7.62 X 54 round into the chamber of the Dragunov SVD and wrapped my hand back around the pistol grip through the skeletonized butt stock.

"What the hell's the range of that thing?" Reed asked from behind me.

Without moving, I murmured, "Maximum effective range is eight hundred meters with the specially selected ammo the gun's issued with. But I don't like a single trigger system on a sniper rifle. And I don't like a semi-automatic in a sniper rifle. And I've never fired a Dragunov before so I don't know what kind of quirks it might have. And if I do fire it, the scope's gonna go banging right into my eye and so my follow-up shot's gonna be slow and likely gonna be off. It uses the same rimmed cartridge they use in their PK GPMG and the RPK LMG-high pressure load. Any more questions?"

"No."

"Then shut up and let me concentrate," I rasped, watching now as Vladov led his men down into the roadway. Vladov would either flag down the approaching sentry vehicle or attempt to stop it on the fly. I settled the scope on the machine gunner in the back of the four wheel drive vehicle. A quick shot would put him away and give Vladov's men a chance to stop the vehicle before getting gunned down.

I waited, suddenly remembering... when Paul and I had taken cover in the rocks above the wreckage of the jet liner and I had used my own sniping rifle against the brigands who were systematically murdering the survivors of the crash. How long ago had it been? I wondered, not consciously wanting to remember.

The vehicle began to slow, the face of the man with the machinegun showed something I could read through the Dragunov's PS0-1sight; suspicion was written all over it.

"Watch out," I said aloud.

CHAPTER ONE HUNDRED SIX

Transcribed from a series of interviews with John Rourke, continued.
<u>**John Rourke is speaking unless otherwise indicated:**</u>

Captain Vladov stood in the middle of the roadway, his right hand raised and waving. The vehicle had already begun to slow. The vehicle ground to a halt, the brakes screeching slightly. Vladov approached the vehicle, the man beside the driver moving his AKM slightly. Vladov kept walking, his men behind him.

He engaged the driver in conversation as he began to draw the Walther PPK/S... the driver started to move his hands on the wheel... the man from the front seat opened his mouth, raising his AKM... the machine gunner was swinging the weapon toward him... the bolt being worked.

I could tell the silencer was stuck in his clothing, he ripped the silencer clear and thrust the pistol forward and pumped the trigger. A neat hole where the right eyebrow of the machine gunner had been. A second round, the bridge of the nose ruptured blood. Vladov swung the silenced Walther to his right but Daszrozinski and Corporal Ravitski were on the man with the AKM, Daszrozinski ripping open the man's throat with a knife.

Ravitski was thrusting a bayonet into the soldier's abdomen. Three of Vladov's men were swarming over the hood of the vehicle toward the driver, but the vehicle was already in motion, moving.

Vladov fired the Walther once, then again and again, into the back of the driver's head and neck. The driver slumped forward. Ravitski had the wheel, leaning across the already dead soldier with the AKM, his hands visibly groping for the emergency brake. The vehicle stopped.

I checked my watch... eight minutes, perhaps less before the next patrol vehicle would be along, very little time.

CHAPTER ONE HUNDRED SEVEN

Transcribed from a series of interviews with John Rourke, continued.
John Rourke is speaking unless otherwise indicated:

Three of Vladov's men were already boarding the sentry vehicle, three others dragging the bodies of the dead to the side of the road.

I saw Natalia, running ahead of the remainder of the American force. If it could be set up properly, I realized, we would have a solid chance against the convoy, but after that... once we reached Cheyenne Mountain and tried to bluff our way in ... I just didn't know. *Have to play it a step at a time,* I thought, *one step at a time.*

*****

I left a small force of Americans and Russians back up into the rocks, with the assault rifles, backpacks and other heavy gear of the remainder of the force.

Natalia, me, Reed, then Sergeant Dressler waited in the drop of the far side of the road from the high rocks. The next patrol had been waved past by Vladov, the Jeep's hood up, Vladov proclaiming a loose battery cable.

Natalia had her silenced stainless Walther back, freshly loaded. For the rest, beyond Natalia's pistol, it was nothing but knives and hands. I had the Gerber Mk 11 fighting knife, the spear point double edged blade given a quick touch up on the sharpening steel carried on the outside of the sheath.

I had my handguns, but no intention of using them. A shot fired would blow the entire operation, because in the mountains as we were, sound would carry for great distances.

We waited, listening for the first rumbling sounds of the convoy. Three trucks, U.S. Army deuce and a halves, and two motorcycle combinations. These were Soviet M-2s, the sidecars fitted with RPK light machineguns with forty-round magazines. There was no way to know what the trucks carried or how many men beyond the two men visible in the truck cabs. We waited.

Then I heard it, the sound of a two and one-half ton truck's gearbox, the roar of an engine. Then the sound of one of the motorcycle combinations. There was a closer sound, the sound of steel being drawn against leather; Sergeant Dressler had what I recognized as a Randall Bowie.

There would be no sound of Natalia's Bali-Song being opened, she would open it when she needed it and not before. It was usually her way.

I pricked my ears, listening as Vladov shouted to the convoy. "There is trouble along the roadway; we must see your papers." There was the screech of brakes, the sounds of transmissions gearing down. "We must see your papers, who commands this convoy?" Vladov's voice.

Another voice, the voice with a heavy Ukrainian accent. "I command this convoy, Corporal, what is the meaning of this? These materials are consigned to The Womb Project."

"I must check your papers, Comrade Major, I am sorry, but I have my orders from Comrade Colonel Rozhdestvenskiy himself, Comrade Major."

"This is preposterous, what sort of trouble along the road?"

"The trouble, Comrade Major, it is very grave. A group of Americans and renegade Russian soldiers have infiltrated the area and are preparing to attack one of the convoys in order to gain entrance to The Womb and sabotage the efforts of our leaders."

"This is criminal, these men, they must be stopped."

"No, Comrade Major, they must not be stopped. Not yet."

"Yet." I jumped up from the rocks, rolling onto the road surface, to my feet now, the Gerber ahead of me like a wand... a wand of death. Vladov scrambled over the roof of the patrol vehicle, jumping, hurtling himself at the KGB officer.

There was a plopping sound from behind me, Natalia's silenced Walther. The AKM armed man beside the KGB officer down before he raised his assault rifle to fire.

I dove the two yards distance to the man standing beside the nearest truck, the blade of the Gerber biting into the throat of the man. I twisted the blade, shoved the body choking to death on blood. I clambered up into the truck cab. The driver was pulling a revolver.

I thrust forward with the knife, hacking literally across the man's throat. Blood spurted from the sliced artery across the interior front windshield. My left hand grabbed at the man's gun hand, finding the revolver. The web of flesh between thumb and first finger interposing between the hammer and the frame as the hammer fell.

It was a Detective Special, and I pocketed the little blued .38 Special, shoved the body out on the driver's side door, rolled back and jumped down to the road on the passenger side, onto the back of a KGB man with an AKM.

I took the man's face in my left hand, as I dropped back, wrenching the head back and slashing the Gerber from left to right across the exposed throat, then ramming it into the right kidney, putting the man down.

Natalia fired the PPK/S, the slide locking back, open as the man in front of her went down from the silenced shot.

She wheeled, the right hand arcing forward, the click-click-click sound of the Bali-Song flashing open, then her right hand punched forward. The Bali-Song puncturing the Adam's apple of the man whom a split second earlier she had hit with the pistol. He fell back. She wheeled right, three men rushed her.

I dove toward them, snatching one man at the shoulder, bulldogging him down, imbedding the Gerber in his the chest, twisted, withdrew.

Natalia's Bali-Song kept opening and closing, it flashed forward, the second of the three men screaming, blood gushing from his throat where she'd opened the artery. I knocked down the third man with a double Ti Kwan Doe kick to the right side of the man's head, the man falling away. She sliced across his gun hand wrist and a Makarov clattered to the road surface along with the last two fingers of his hand.

I stepped toward the man, my right foot catching him at the base of the nose, breaking it, driving the bone up and through and into the brain.

The fighting had stopped. Vladov stood there a few yards from me, Reed was beside him, both men's knives glinted red with blood in the sunlight. The convoy personnel lay dead and dying.

"No casualties," Reed murmured. "Looks like anyway."

"Many casualties," Vladov corrected. "Too many, I think."

CHAPTER ONE HUNDRED EIGHT

Transcribed from a series of interviews with John Rourke, continued. <u>John Rourke is speaking unless otherwise indicated:</u>

The trucks were rolling. Vladov and Daszrozinski manned the M-72 combinations, two of the Soviet SFers riding the sidecars to man the RPK LMGs. I drove the first truck, my Russian was good enough I thought and Natalia had confirmed.

Beside me, she was changing into the smallest of the Soviet enlisted men's uniform we could find. "If I'd wanted a uniform, I could have brought my own uniform."

"Yeah. But the Russians don't use women for details like this, and besides, dressed like a woman you're too recognizable to the KGB."

"You shouldn't have ridden in the front truck in the convoy."

"Didn't have any choice," she laughed. "I wanted to be with you and besides, you're the only man here I'd undress in front of."

"I don't know if that's a compliment or not," I told her, looking at her for an instant. "If we get out of this, we can get the cryogenic chambers we can steal and the serum, we can get it to the Retreat. Maybe get Vladov and some of his men there and Reed and some of his men... could accommodate more than the six of us. And you can get things ready, I can go after your uncle and Catherine and try and get them out."

"No."

"Why not?"

"Because you'd be killed, it's as simple as that. There are three people I care for in the world. I've resigned myself to losing my uncle. But I won't risk losing either of the other two, yourself, Paul. If you go, Paul will go too, you know that. When I looked at his wound I realized he'd be at full capacity in another few days, by the time we get back, if we get back, when we get back, you won't be able to stop him.

"No, I love my uncle, he's the only real parent I ever had, but I won't let you die trying to bring him back. He's ready to die; he feels he's lived his life. I don't accept that, but I respect it. You'd never get him out alive.

"If we pull this off, if we destroy The Womb's capabilities to survive the holocaust, if we steal the chambers and the cryogenic serum we need and destroy the rest... if any of Rozhdestvenskiy's men survive, they won't rest until they hunt you down or the fire consumes them. You'd never reach Chicago; you'd never get out of the city if you did.

"I won't let you go, if I have to shoot your kneecaps to stop you, I won't let you leave me."

I didn't know what to say to her.

CHAPTER ONE HUNDRED NINE

Transcribed from historical artifacts of the government of U.S. II located in an archaeological dig, in area formerly identified as Texas. <u>President Chambers is speaking unless otherwise indicated:</u>

I cleared my throat and said, "We must assume that Lieutenant Feltcher never made contact with the TVM, so we're in this thing against the KGB and the Army units under their control all alone." He studied the faces of his officers and senior noncoms. He looked away from them, trying to search for the right words. "I...I don't know what to say. I was never a politician. I was a scientist basically; I guess that was all I ever wanted to be. As your president, I should be able to say something consoling, something inspirational to you at this time.

"The Russians are closing in from both flanks, we have enough aircraft to evacuate some key personnel, but there isn't any point to it. At dawn today, I considered the fact that God had given us another day of life.

"But, dawn tomorrow... the next day or within a few days after that, the world will end. As a scientist, I couldn't confirm or deny any of the hypotheses formed for post-war scenarios. But the Supreme Soviet Commander, General Varakov, had access to scientific data.

"Who do we blame? Scientists for creating these weapons, the military for using them, the governments for ordering their use? The truth is that I don't know who to blame. I blame myself as an individual matter of conscience. And maybe each of us should do that.

"So, God gave us this extra day. It's clear our Soviet adversaries don't know of the coming holocaust. I think it's up to us to use this day in the defense of an ideal that somehow, even after all mankind is dead, somewhere there is a spark that won't die. I'm talking about liberty. That's all I have to say besides God bless us all."

It started with one man, then another and then still another, hands clapped to applause, but as the first and last president of United States II, the applause were not for the words he had uttered, but for the feelings the words echoed from the hearts of the Americans he stood before. Unashamed, as I stood there beneath the rafters, I wept.

CHAPTER ONE HUNDRED TEN

Transcribed from a series of interviews with John Rourke. <u>John Rourke speaking unless otherwise indicated:</u>

Things were a little... intense. Lieutenant Daszrozinski, Vladov's second in command, was wearing the uniform of a dead KGB major. And Corporal Ravitski wore the uniform of the slain lieutenant of the KGB. The Americans were hidden in the trucks, unfortunately behind cases of C-4. Natalia beside me, in male drag, the uniform of a corporal, said, "What do you think?"

"About what?"

"Will we make it inside, I mean?"

I shrugged. "Tell you one thing, keep your mouth shut beyond a yes or no, you've got girl all over your voice. And watch your eyes, squint or something. They see those, they'll figure something's wrong."

"Why don't I just hide in the back of the truck?"

"Because if there is a fight, you're better than anybody else."

"Except you, maybe."

"Maybe," I said and glanced at her and laughed. "That's another thing that'll blow your disguise," I murmured. "Holding my hand." She started to take her hand away, but I held it tight. "But I'll tell you when it gets dangerous and you have to stop."

While that was hardly a "light moment," it proved to be the last one we had for some time.

*****

Daszrozinski and Ravitski passed the sentry box between the first and second fence. Because of increased security restrictions, we had to leave the shipment beyond the primary doors to the receiving area. From there, Womb personnel would take over the vehicles. We were to wait in a rest area in a tent near the airfield while the cargo was being unloaded. We passed under the lintel of the bombproof doors. I saw the vault door leading into The Womb itself. It was open as it should be. It was time...

CHAPTER ONE HUNDRED ELEVEN

Transcribed from a series of interviews with John Rourke continued. <u>John Rourke is speaking unless otherwise indicated:</u>

There was not an AK type weapon to be seen, the KGB personnel all carried M-16s and those few personnel who carried side arms wore .45s, the "U.S." symbols on the flaps of the holsters.

Following a Sergeant's directions, I aimed the nose of the deuce and a half toward the loading dock area. I started backing the vehicle toward the loading dock. Vladov had to make his move quickly. Once the first of the boxes was moved, the Americans inside the truck would be spotted. I told Vladov, "Tell the convoy personnel to disembark the vehicles. When they holler at you for it, tell them the men are tired from the drive and you're going to rest them, you out rank everyone I've seen out here."

He did and everyone got out and made a show of stretching. It would be a lot easier to fight being already out of the trucks and standing. The loading dock personnel approached the trucks. It was time.

Each of the Americans carried five pounds of the C-4, liberated from the packing crates, the rest of the C-4 in the three trucks was wired to detonate, the charges positioned to blow outward toward the flanking trucks and detonate the plastique there. The last man out the trucks had left a wristwatch commandeered from one of the dead KGB men beside the battery, set for two minutes.

As the loading dock personnel started to lift the tarp, Vladov shouted in Russian, then in English, "We attack!" The vault door to The Womb stood open... it started to close.

All hell broke loose.

CHAPTER ONE HUNDRED TWELVE

Transcribed from a series of interviews with John Rourke, continued. <u>John Rourke is speaking unless otherwise indicated:</u>

I lost count of the number of men we killed and I lost count of the men we lost. It was kill or be killed, live or die and some of us were going to live and hopefully... all of them were going to die.

I commandeered a Jeep and drove it hard against the closing vault door, jumping clear as the Jeep hit. The vault door bit into the Jeep, partially crushing it, but the vault door was open at least three feet. I shouted for Reed and Daszrozinski to get their men through the doorway. I had lost sight of Vladov.

CHAPTER ONE HUNDRED THIRTEEN

Transcribed from automatic wire recordings located in an archaeological dig at the former Cheyenne Mountain complex and interviews with John Rourke. One of the speakers is Nehemiah Rozhdestvenskiy, Commander of the North American Branch of the Committee for State Security of the Soviet:

Rozhdestvenskiy: "What is happening, Major Revnik?"

Revnik: "A group of men, and one woman, have entered The Womb. They have detonated explosives at the loading dock, many of our men are killed, Comrade Colonel."

Rozhdestvenskiy: "Who are they?"

Revnik: "I do not know, some of them seem Russian, some of them are dressed in American uniforms, Comrade Colonel."

"Comrade Colonel Rozhdestvenskiy," another voice said. "I recognized the woman from my tour of duty in Chicago. It is Comrade Major Tiemerovna."

Rozhdestvenskiy: "And the man, one of the men with her must be Rourke."

Revnik: "The doctor whom you have sought, Comrade Colonel?"

Rozhdestvenskiy: "Yes! Damn his eyes. Revnik, get me fifty of our best men, assemble them here. I shall take charge of dispatching this Rourke and the traitorous Major Tiemerovna myself."

CHAPTER ONE HUNDRED FOURTEEN

**Transcribed from a series of interviews with John Rourke, continued.
<u>John Rourke is speaking unless otherwise indicated:</u>**

Vladov suddenly appeared, with a dark blue beret on his head, at a rakish angle. I said, "We've got two jobs, to knock out the particle beam weapons so they can't be repaired at all. Then we've got to locate the cryogenics laboratory, destroy the cryogenic serum and sabotage the life support systems for The Womb and anything else."

Vladov nodded. "And you are to steal as many of the cryogenic chambers as possible, this is General Varakov's directive to save yourself and the major and your family, and perhaps some of the men who fight with Colonel Reed."

"And, the men who fight with you," I corrected.

"Them as well," Vladov replied.

"What the hell do you mean?" It was Reed, and as if punctuating his remarks, small arms fire began to erupt from the far side of the vaulted stone hall beyond the interior bombproof vault door.

Vladov turned to Reed. "It may be possible, Colonel, that some of your men or my men may find sanctuary at Doctor Rourke's mountain Retreat and survive the holocaust. But I suggest there is little time to argue. And I suggest that it is more likely the case none of us shall leave this place alive."

The gunfire was increasing in volume. Reed nodded, "At least I agree with ya on that, Captain."

I interrupted the discussion. "We have to get past their position to the left, if General Varakov had his information right. A long corridor, it should be a shooting gallery."

Chapter One Hundred Fifteen

Transcribed from automatic wire recordings located in an archaeological dig at the former Cheyenne Mountain complex. The primary speaker is <u>Nehemiah Rozhdestvenskiy</u>, Commander of the North American Branch of the Committee for State Security of the Soviet:

Rozhdestvenskiy: "Attention all personnel. This is Colonel Nehemiah Rozhdestvenskiy. The Womb is under siege from within. Approximately two dozen American saboteurs and Soviet traitors. Their objective is to reach the cryogenics laboratory and to destroy our very chances of survival. They are to be stomped out like the vermin that they are. They would destroy our plans for world order in the future. They are our enemies. All personnel, male or female, are to be armed. Ninety rounds of ammunition per weapon. The arsenal rooms are then to be locked and secured and guarded. Hunt these traitors and saboteurs, hunt them down and kill them. But if at all possible, two of them are to be brought to me alive. The sole woman, Major Natalia Tiemerovna, the niece of Comrade General Varakov who must have been tricked into giving her secret information concerning The Womb. She is also the treacherous widow of our late spiritual leader Vladimir Karamatsov, a hero to us all, in whose memory we still serve.

"The other a man, American. He is tall, muscular appearing. He reportedly habitually carries two small, stainless steel finish .45 caliber pistols in a double shoulder holster. His name is Dr. John Rourke. He is a terrorist with the American Central Intelligence Agency. The person responsible for bringing one or both of these persons to me alive shall be awarded the highest honors and hold great responsibility and influence in the new order that shall be formed after the awakening. This is my word. I shall personally lead a search and destroy unit in pursuit of these enemies. Find them. Stop them. Kill them. Bring Dr. Rourke and Major Tiemerovna to me, alive."

CHAPTER ONE HUNDRED SIXTEEN

Transcribed from a series of interviews with John Rourke. <u>John Rourke is speaking unless otherwise indicated:</u>

Nine of Reed's men survived along with Reed and eleven of Vladov's men.

Reed said, "If this is the terminus between the cryogenics lab and the particle beam installation, then this is where we part company, Rourke. We're runnin' out of time. All this creep Rozhdestvenskiy has to do is get lucky and intercept us in one of the passageways with a vastly superior force and we're goners. I'm taking my men up top to knock out the particle beam weapons."

"My assigned task, I believe," Vladov said, "is the destruction of the cryogenics laboratory."

"If either group is successful," Natalia began, "the KGB master plan will be severely damaged."

"If both groups are successful, we'll knock 'em out of the box," I nodded. "All right, we split up. Natalia and I are heading for the cryogenics lab, if somehow I can get some of those cryogenic chambers and enough of the serum, well... maybe there's a chance for my family to survive this. I'll give you the location of the Retreat, Reed, you can..."

"I'm never getting out of here alive. I walked in here knowing that. I think Captain Vladov feels the same way. The more of these KGB assholes we kill, well, the bigger the smile on my face when the bullet finds me."

"My sentiments as well, Colonel," Vladov smiled.

"You can't say that," I told Reed. "You might make it out."

"I'd head back for Texas if I did. KGB units and Army units under their control should be pounding the hell out of our boys right now."

"And I," Vladov smiled. "Someone must stay behind to destroy all that is in here, so that if some of mankind does survive, no one will be able to use this place and the material here to establish himself as a dictator. No, once the primary mission is finished, we shall continue to sabotage all that can be destroyed here in The Womb."

I extended my hand to Reed. "I won't lie and say I've enjoyed knowing you, but I respect you. Good luck, and God bless you, too." Reed took my hand, nodded, saying nothing.

Vladov extended his hand to Reed. "Colonel, I think at least we are fully allies."

Reed's eyes flickered, and then he released my hand and took Vladov's. "Captain, my sincerest respect to you, to Lieutenant Daszrozinski, your men. Godspeed, Captain."

"And to you, Colonel." Vladov took a step back and saluted. Reed hesitated, then drew himself up and returned the salute, holding it for a long moment, then dropping it, Vladov turning away and walking back toward the pickup truck.

Reed looked at Natalia and me. "I never figured out either of you. Figured Rourke was crazy for not jumpin' your bones, Major, no offense. I would have. So I guess that's a compliment. And you, Rourke, so fuckin' independent, always so damned right, so damned perfect. I guess about the best compliment I can give and I mean it. You're a good American and we could've used more like you."

Natalia took two hesitant steps forward, leaned up and kissed Reed on the cheek. Reed looked at her and smiled. "Major, if you don't mind a dying man getting his last request?"

She didn't answer him. Reed put his hands on her upper arms and drew her toward him, then kissed her full on the lips, she kissed him back.

"I was right all along," Reed smiled, letting go of her. "Rourke, he was crazy all this time, lady." Colonel Reed turned away and started to walk, quickly, erect toward the knot of his men ten yards away.

He never looked back.

CHAPTER ONE HUNDRED SEVENTEEN

Transcribed from historical artifacts of the government of U.S. II located in an archaeological dig, in area formerly identified as Texas:

"Halversen," President Chambers shouted, calling to the radio man at the far end of the bunker. "Halversen!"

"Mr. President, nothing yet. I've tried every frequency that the KGB hasn't jammed. If the Texans are coming, Sir, well they aren't receiving us at all and I'm not picking up any of their talk."

Chambers turned away, rasping, "Keep trying, Halversen."

"Where the hell's the president?" asked a young man in Air Force fatigues leaning in through the door.

"Who wants him, Sergeant?"

"My lieutenant told me to run over here. The last of the surface to air missiles was fired." There was the sound of an explosion from outside, then more gunfire. "They send any more of them damn MiG airplanes against our position, we're goners."

"They send too many more against this whole Army, we're goners."

"Where the hell's the president... supposed to tell him personally."

"Be back in a minute," Chambers said, glancing toward Halversen, but the radio man's head was leaned toward his machine.

"Probably off stickin' his head in some goddamned hole figurin' he's gonna get shot."

Chambers smiled. "Or maybe he dressed up like a woman and tried to escape through the lines, like Santa Anna did after he lost to Houston at the Battle of San Jacinto."

The Air Force sergeant laughed. "Naw, everything I hear, well, Chambers, he's a good old boy, even for a scientist, or a president. But I gotta find him though. Lieutenant wants to know what to do."

"You found him, son, I'm the president."

"You, why..." and the young Air Force Sergeant, he looked barely older than nineteen, but promotion had come fast during the weeks since the Night of The War, snapped to attention. "I'm sorry, Sir... I..."

"You tell your lieutenant that when the SAMs are gone to get every man in his battery to pick up an assault rifle off one of the men who's already dead. When the Russian planes come, have him have all of you fire in volleys toward the weapons pods underneath the wings. If the weapons are armed and you get a lucky hit, you might activate a detonator and blow up the damned plane. Move out, Sergeant."

"Yes, Sir," and the man started to go, then turned back.

"I'm sorry for what I said, Mr. President, about the damn hole and all."

"It was a goddamned hole and no offense taken. Good luck, Sergeant."

CHAPTER ONE HUNDRED EIGHTEEN

Transcribed from conversation between John Rourke and myself, Paul Rubenstein:

Paul Rubenstein: "Did you ever see Reed again?"

John shook his head. "No, not him or Sergeant Dressler or Tom Maus or the Resistance Fighters. But we saw the result of their efforts. With Reed it was the particle beam weapons on the top of the mountain that told the story.

"If Reed and his men hadn't knocked out the particle beam weapons, I'd have never gotten the cryogenic chambers or any of the serum out of there. They would have blown my aircraft out of the sky. It was imperative that some of the folks with me survived to get back to the Retreat and you and Sarah and the kids."

Paul Rubenstein: "Because someone needed to be alive to warn the returning Eden Project, to tell the story of what happened."

Rourke frowned. "Yeah... naw... yeah. It gets complicated, Paul. Part of me was only concerned with us; you, Sarah, the kids, Natalia and me, making it. Yet, at the same time I felt an imperative that someone make it to be able to tell the story at least."

Paul Rubenstein: "I understand, those were my two imperatives. Frankly, I wasn't that sure about the Eden Project. I knew a lot could go wrong with that. A malfunction in the onboard electrical systems could cause the cryogenic chambers inside the shuttles to quit. Or a meteor shower might destroy them. An incorrect mathematical calculation... instead of an elliptical orbit... they might instead drift out of the solar system and sail on forever.

"If they woke up, they would be doomed to wander forever... if they chose to return to their sleep, or they would die in a matter of days when shipboard oxygen was depleted. In other words, the survival of us was vital. For sure, without us there would be no human race and all of mankind would have been lost."

Rourke: "I suspected that some people might survive, living underground, if they were strong enough and technologically set. But yes... I thought our family the best bet for the survival of the human race."

Paul Rubenstein: "Human race... I remember the story you told me about Vladov saying the name of his unit meant 'Fight' and he had asked for a street or village square have that name in the new world if there was to be one."

Rourke: "Human race... yes a village square where children could play. And that somehow, some way, his people might know it. A Russian name... a Russian word in an American town. How fitting for the human race."

Paul Rubenstein: "It still amazes me how everything came to a crescendo that day."

Rourke: "Yeah, so many things going right, but it was too late in the end. So many things going wrong but working anyway."

Paul Rubenstein: "As I learned more about it all... it seemed preordained. Like Lieutenant Feltcher finally arriving at the battle in Texas."

Rourke: "I remember when Vladov and his men had first moved out, Natalia had changed into her own clothes, her battle gear, a black jump suit. I too changed out of the borrowed Soviet uniform, back to my Levis, combat boots, shirt, and bomber jacket covering the Detonics pistols. Hell was breaking out again.

"Natalia and I headed to where Vladov's men were pinned down by Rozhdestvenskiy's men. Vladov shouted, 'Get out of here, Doctor. You and the Major must be about your business.' I shouted, 'Vladov, God bless you!' He shouted back, 'And you!'"

Paul Rubenstein: "You were headed for the cryogenics lab?"

Rourke: "Yeah, when we got in there, probably everyone was dead or dying. The far wall was dominated by rows of shelves, three liter sized bottles, the color of the bottles a very pale green, like the color of Rhine wine."

Paul Rubenstein: "The cryogenic serum?"

Rourke: "Yeah, and to my left running the length of the laboratory, were the cryogenic chambers. Some translucent lids open, some closed, monitoring equipment rigged to them and alongside their wooden packing crates.

"I heard a sound and a panel in the ceiling slid open, the muzzles of automatic rifles pointed down at us. A voice said, 'Doctor Rourke, a moment, please!' That bastard, Rozhdestvenskiy, wanted to chat. We were trapped.

"Natalia stopped the bastard. She raised her rifles, she said, 'The muzzles of both rifles are packed with C-4 explosives, one pound apiece. All I have to do is twitch my finger against either trigger and the explosions will destroy the cryogenic serum for you.'

"I said, 'Even if your gunfire should sever her arms from her body, the involuntary nervous responses will cause the fingers to twitch against the triggers. Your serum, your life... all gone. We came here for some of the cryogenic chambers and monitoring equipment, and a supply of serum for ourselves... and to destroy your serum. So you'd die when the holocaust comes. We'll settle for some of the chambers, six. We'll take six along with the spare parts kits, the monitoring equipment. We'll take six bottles of the serum.

"I had the Russians load us up with six of the U.S. made cryogenic chambers I had personally inspected. Six spare parts kits. Six monitoring equipment kits, six spare parts kits for the monitoring equipment. Five of the serum bottles, packed in wooden cases were aboard the truck and Natalia was bringing the sixth bottle.

"We got out of The Womb, but the bastard came after us. I could have destroyed the serum, but I needed it to keep all of you alive. I found a plane, a modified Grumman OV-1 Mohawk of the type used in Vietnam. We had to make it back to the prototype jet fighter. I didn't think we could.

"There was an explosion, louder than anything I had ever heard before, the top of the mountain, a mushroom shaped ball of fire rising skyward. Reed..."

CHAPTER ONE HUNDRED NINETEEN

This information was transcribed by <u>Colonel Nehemiah Rozhdestvenskiy</u>, Commander of the North American Branch of The Committee for State Security of the Soviet and discovered at an archaeological dig at the former Cheyenne Mountain complex:

Report # 67206/Personal: I stare at the mountain without a top, my mountain that no longer could be hermetically sealed, The Womb was now useless to me. Captain Andreki is babbling we must escape before the radiation can reach the airfield.

Rourke will die for this. I ordered all radar installations which still function to search for his plane. All ground forces are to search for it. We shall take whatever means at our disposal and go to northeastern Georgia. We shall search the mountains there throughout the night. We shall find this Retreat, we shall destroy it, destroy Rourke and Major Tiemerovna, destroy Rourke's family. We shall have the last victory.

Signed

<original signed>
Nehemiah Rozhdestvenskiy, Colonel. Commander of the North American Branch of The Committee for State Security of the Soviet.

CHAPTER ONE HUNDRED TWENTY

Transcribed from artifacts located in an archaeological dig, in area formerly identified as the Museum of Natural History, Chicago. <u>Primary speaker is General Ishmael Varakov:</u>

"General Ishmael Varakov," Catherine said, "Moscow is gone. The radio was full of static and then for an instant it cleared. All the radio operator could say was 'fire', then there was nothing more, not even static."

I told her it has begun and she should stand beside me and we shall talk. "You can tell me of your childhood perhaps. We have one night in which to tell each other all that we might ever wish to tell each other. Let us look at the two fighting mastodons for a while, for the last time." She left to "pretty up" as she called it. She will be back shortly.

My feet hurt.

There was the First World War, which was to be the war to end all wars, but so many of our soldiers never returned and then the era of Kerenski, and that failed, and then Lenin finally took charge and there was fighting everywhere.

Then came the Second World War, in which I fought, Stalin was a fool to ever trust the Nazis. They turned on us and tried to destroy us and later we destroyed them. All this, you would think, that with all the millions who died in the First War, the many who died during the Revolution, the millions who died during the Second War, you would think that we would have learned something.

Something to tell young people that would magically make them understand how stupid and useless it all was. But did we?

When she comes back I shall look into ·her eyes and say, "You are a pretty young girl. I do not still understand why you would so favor an old man by loving him, but I am glad that you do. Sit and tell me about your childhood."

We will sit near the feet of the mastodons, Catherine sitting beside me. "I did nothing interesting, Comrade General," she shall say as she always does. "It is a very boring story, there is nothing interesting about me..."

And I will hold her hand and say as I always do, "How wrong you are, my child. How incredibly wrong you are."

*****

My Reflection:

I have often worried about General Ishmael Varakov and his last moments in this world. He was a good man, a great man; he remains part of the Rourke family to this day. Every year in October, we still gather to celebrate his birthday.

I like to think that at the end, he found a love story with Catherine. Not the love story he had with Natalia's mother; a man only has that once in his life. Rather a love story that was sweet and innocent and warm and that he died with.

In my mind's eye, I envision him behind the figures of the mastodons, his left arm folded around Catherine's shoulders as they waited. His thoughts on his niece Natalia and the girl beside him who loved him.

I believe he would have thought of God... if there was God... and he would have hoped there was.

Outside he would be able to hear the thunder. Outside he would have seen the lightning in the storm blackened sky... destruction and beauty co-mingled.

I know he had found honor, I believe he had found love in many places and I believe he had found what he felt was truth.

He would have held Catherine more closely to him when he saw it... the wave of flames that belched through the open brass doors of the museum, washed over and through the mastodons. He would not have screamed as the fire engulfed them; it would have scared Catherine.

No one will ever know... there are no records. But I have that scene in my dreams from time to time and as someone said, long ago, before The Night of the War... "A dream is a wish your heart makes."

Like General Varakov, our lives, the Rourke Family, did not turn out the way we thought they would. Even today, the twists and turns continue to amaze me. Ours, unlike Varakov's, remain flexible, ever changing, fluid... after all we are all still alive.

CHAPTER ONE HUNDRED TWENTY-ONE

Transcribed from a series of interviews with John Rourke. <u>John Rourke is speaking unless otherwise indicated:</u>

I landed the aircraft on a stretch of straight highway, then taxied it off the road and into a field until it was unable to go further. Natalia went on ahead, to the original takeoff site we had used with the prototype fighter. My Harley was hidden there. I worked while she had been gone, getting the eighteen smaller crates offloaded from the plane, getting the six coffin shaped crates which contained the cryogenic chambers nearer to the hatch.

I had field stripped the guns one at a time, cleaning them. I had touched up the edges of my knives; basically I did anything to avoid thinking.

It was already the new day beyond the ocean and soon... I somehow knew that it was the last day. A plan had already formed, a plan to solve that which was unsolvable. But it meant putting myself in the position of God, and it was an uncomfortable thought.

I loved Sarah and I loved Natalia. I loved them equally, at least I told myself that, and I loved them differently. It was the only way to solve it.

If all went well and we were able to utilize the cryogenics equipment and the last precious bottle of the serum, we would survive. But we only had that one bottle; all the rest had been destroyed escaping from The Womb, such a loss. If all went well, I would sleep for nearly five centuries. If it did not go well, I... we... would die. In either event, sleep now was unimportant. Waking up was our primary goal.

I heard the sound of the trucks, the familiar sound of my own camouflaged Ford pickup truck. The less familiar sounds of the truck I had borrowed from Pete Critchfield, the Resistance leader.

I wondered if Natalia had told Paul and Sarah and the children what would happen at the next dawn. Had she told Paul the story Reed had recounted of the death of Paul's parents? I doubted she had, it was, after all, my responsibility.

CHAPTER ONE HUNDRED TWENTY-TWO

Transcribed from historical artifacts of the government of U.S. II located in an archaeological dig, in area formerly identified as Texas. <u>President Chambers is speaking unless otherwise indicated:</u>

I stood on the rise of ground looking out. I could see much by the fires that still burned. Beside me stood Lieutenant Feltcher, he and his men had finally arrived. I had feared he would be my Fannin and I would be his Travis.

Travis waited at the Alamo for Fannin and almost 400 troops to arrive not knowing Colonel James Walker Fannin, Jr. and nearly all of his men had been executed at Goliad, Texas. But my Fannin, Feltcher and his men, had arrived and the Soviet Armies had been defeated... routed.

Feltcher said, "We won, Mr. President. My radio man has been getting these weird signals all night. Ham operators, like that."

"I know, all victory is fleeting."

"What do you mean, Sir?"

I looked at Feltcher. I didn't have the heart to tell him. Instead, I said, "Maybe what transpired will bring about peace someday. Maybe somebody somewhere will look back and know what happened, maybe."

"You mean, Mr. President, maybe we whipped them so bad we'll really beat them, drive 'em back to the Soviet Union, have America back?"

"By tomorrow morning, I'm confident of it, Lieutenant, all our troubles will be over."

"Is it some new weapon, Sir?"

I looked at Feltcher in the firelight, then just shook my head as I lit a cigarette; I had several packs to still smoke that night. There was no sense wasting the last of my cigarettes.

"No, not a new weapon, Lieutenant. I think we'll shortly see the old weapons did quite enough, quite enough." I inhaled the smoke deep into my lungs and said nothing else for a moment.

Then I looked at Feltcher. "While you were away, well, it's too long a story. But I'll tell you anyway. We did something to the air and the sky is catching on fire and when the sun rises tomorrow morning we'll all be dead. And there's no way to stop it.

"I've got a lot of smoking to do, if you want to join me, I'll tell you about it. Or maybe you want to find someplace to go and pray. Up to you, Lieutenant."

Feltcher didn't say anything. After a moment there was a solitary pistol shot. Someone in the darkness, I knew, had just taken his own life rather than face the sunrise. Others had already, others would.

I began to walk toward the tent that was my newest headquarters, my last headquarters. I turned around to look at Feltcher. The young lieutenant was making the sign of the cross.

Transcribed from a series of interviews with Natalia Tiemerovna. <u>Natalia is speaking unless otherwise indicated:</u>

It was a busy time, the children served as "gophers", go for this and go for that. Paul, with Michael's help had prepared the bikes and the trucks for the long term storage. Sarah, with Annie's help, had prepared the foodstuffs and supervised the plants which renewed the oxygen supply inside the Retreat.

They would not last the five hundred years, but with the timer connected grow lights and water sprays, they would thrive long enough that when we awakened in five hundred years... if we awakened, the oxygen would be clean to breathe if not very fresh.

We had seen to all of the weapons, seen to the generator systems, the back-up generators, all these keyed to the hydroelectric power system based on the underground stream and the waterfall. If it failed, the cryogenic chambers would be our coffins and we would never awaken.

The last of the cables were being strung, linking the cryogenic chambers' monitoring systems to the power supply, Annie feeding cable while I connected it. John stepped to the electronic monitoring console. There had never been a need for the system before. But we had activated it once we had sealed the main entrance of the Retreat.

The two escape chambers had also been checked, John did this himself. The one tunnel leading through to the other side of the mountain was hermetically sealed, as was the main entrance. He had not yet hermetically sealed the second tunnel which led above.

John studied the console controls, then looked up to the television monitoring screen, closed circuit, via cable, it would function until the end, until the atmosphere caught fire and the camera and cable just simply burned.

It was nearly dawn. He adjusted the monitor. In the distance near the base of the mountain, he could make out large numbers of troops moving with mechanized equipment. In the air were helicopters of every description. These were Rozhdestvenskiy's forces, searching for the Retreat to destroy it.

The sun was almost rising; we had worked throughout the night... until we could take no more of it. We listened to shortwave broadcasts, the horror, the devastation. It followed the sun.

There had been a ham operator in Greenland who had constantly been broadcasting, about the fires which consumed Europe. But now even he was silent. There had been other broadcasts, U.S. II announcing the victory over the Soviet Forces.

"John, all set!" I said.

"Good, Paul, help Natalia with the injections."

"I'm through here, too," Sarah called out. "I can help; I've used hypodermics before."

In the monitor, the sky above the Retreat was almost black, lightning bolts streaking across it, ball lightning, pure electricity-shooting in low arcs under the clouds. Men and equipment were moving toward the mountain road.

John exhaled hard, "The injections are ready, all six. Isn't much time left. From the way that sky looks, the ionization is already starting. I'll check the last escape hatch and seal it before I put myself under, give everybody the injections first," he said softly.

Rourke walked the few paces to the coffee table; he looked down at the six hypodermic needles on a white towel there. There was a taped name on each. He picked up the needle for Michael.

"Natalia, you checked my figures, you agree on the amount of the injections."

"There were only tables for body weights down to ninety pounds, John, I worked back through the formula in the manuals accompanying the chambers, Michael weighs sixty-two pounds. The injection should be right," I said.

John looked at the injection, then at his son. "Michael, kiss your mother and sister and then come over to me."

I was beside John in an instant, reaching up, taking the hypodermic from his fingers. "I'll give your son the injection; if something... it shouldn't be your guilt, John." He started to say something, but didn't, just nodding. He watched Michael and his mother hug each other, then watched Annie throw her arms around her brother, kissing him. Michael walked toward him.

Rourke looked down at the boy. "Michael, it should seem like only a little time. I know five hundred years sounds like a long time, but when you're just sleeping..."

"Will I dream a lot, Daddy?"

John dropped to his knees in front of the boy, squeezing Michael tight against him, and as he spoke his voice sounded choked, strained to me. "Son, you'll dream good dreams, I know you will."

I could see the boy's body tense, as the needle entered his son's arm. "I feel...I feel." Rourke stood up, sweeping his son into his arms as the boy fell almost instantly asleep.

"That's supposed to..." I began.

John looked at me, "I know, it's supposed to happen."

John carried his son to the cryogenic chamber, resting the tiny body inside it. His eyes flicked from the elapsed time readout setting back to his son's face.

The breathing was shallow, too shallow? Rourke listened for the heart beat with a stethoscope from the small shelf at the side of the chamber. "It's slow, very slow..."

Sarah was beside him, holding John's arm. Annie, her voice odd sounding, asked, "Is Michael all right?"

"Michael's all right."

*****

Both children rested under the glowing translucent domes now, their faces bathed in the blue light, clouds of gas beginning to swirl around them. John stared at them, Sarah stood on his right with John's arm around her. I stood at his left, my hand in his. Paul by my side.

For the last two minutes, the horror show had continued, the Soviet soldiers as they marched up the mountainside were dying, struck by lightning, ball lightning consumed some of them, human torches. Only three of the helicopters remained aloft, burning debris dotting the landscape. "You'd think they'd give up," John said.

"Would you?" I asked softly.

John said nothing for a long moment, then, "Paul, you're..."

"Yeah, I know. I kind of figured... God," and Paul let out a long, deep breath. "Guess I'd better lie down, in my chamber, huh?"

"Relax, Paul," John whispered, taking the needle, starting toward his friend.

I embraced Paul, kissing him on the lips. Paul stepped back, looking somehow embarrassed.

"I'm going to feel, funny. I'm, aw, just give it to me," Paul said and started to sit down on the edge of his chamber.

John extended his hand, the younger man taking it. "Paul, if I'd had a brother, it would have been you."

The younger man smiled. "I love ya, both of you," and he looked at me then back at John. Already he was rolling up his left sleeve.

"Loosen your belt, kick off your shoes, don't want to constrict your blood vessels. Probably should all be naked."

"I don't think it'll make much difference, if we live, we live. You taught me that," Paul smiled.

"Until we wake up then."

"I always hated shots; let me look the other way."

John gave him the injection. Outside, the electrical storm had intensified still more as John studied the monitor for a moment.

"What are our chances?" I asked John.

"Natural granite will insulate against electrical shock, should keep the air from burning in here. After we're all in the chambers, we won't need air anyway. We'll breathe the gas, it's continuously purified. The plants over there will keep growing," and he gestured beyond the far end of the great room, the plastic covered greenhouse there with the purple grow lights.

"The underground springs should keep up our electrical power. Those grow lights should burn for years with the timers before the fluorescent tubes die, the plants will clean the air we breathe now so there'll be clean air inside the Retreat when we awaken."

"Stale, but it'll be clean. Nothing else on earth, unless it's sealed in granite, nothing should survive, live. We have the only chambers that will work because we have the only serum."

"The Eden Project..."

"If there wasn't a meteor shower that got their hulls, or there wasn't a malfunction in their solar batteries, or something else no one foresaw, they will be back after we awaken."

"I feel like the harlot or something," I glanced at Sarah.

"Don't."

"After we wake up, what?"

"Don't worry, but I know I'm glad you're with me, here."

"Give me the injection, John, unless you want me to administer the injection to Sarah, for you."

"You sleep," John said and kissed me. "I love you." He gave me the injection.

CHAPTER ONE HUNDRED TWENTY-FOUR

Transcribed from interview with John Rourke. <u>John Rourke is speaking unless otherwise indicated:</u>

Sarah stood beside me. "Thank you for finding us, I think." She smiled oddly. "We'll have lot to talk about, the children and other things. You'd better hurry now."

"You always talked us to death," I whispered, chilling at the word. I drew her into my arms, looked into her face, then kissed her.

"What are you going to do, about us?" she whispered back, kissing me again.

"Trust me once more?"

"I love you, John Rourke, and I know you love me. Whatever we make of our lives if we wake up, I guess it doesn't matter as much as our loving one another. We should never have married, we both know that. But I love you."

I walked with her to her chamber. "Will you be all right, can you get your chamber started after you..."

"I'll give myself the injection just after I start my chamber," I assured her. "I can hold my breath against the gas, I'll be fine."

"I know that," she smiled, leaning up to me, kissing me, holding my hand. "I'll see you in five hundred years." She closed her eyes and sat on the edge of her chamber as I put the needle to her skin.

"I love you," I whispered, and as she sank back, asleep.

**Transcribed from interview with John Rourke, continued. <u>John Rourke is
speaking unless otherwise indicated:</u>**

They were all asleep and I studied the television monitor. Perhaps a hundred of the KGB troopers remained now, huddled on the ground, lightning smashing into the rocks beside which they took shelter. "Armageddon," I whispered. Two of the helicopters remained airborne, the sky around them alive with electricity.

"Rozhdestvenskiy," I said, staring at the monitor as one of the helicopters flew near the camera. The sky was black, electricity filling the air, arcing across the ground now. I thought of Reed and what he had died doing.

The double Alessi rig still across my shoulders as I ran the length of the darkened Great Room, the bluish glow of the chambers chilling, eerie somehow. I studied their faces in the chambers, one-by-one, the eyelids closed, the swirling gases marking the faces then seeming to whisk aside.

"I have to," I said to them. "I have to do this, show the KGB why they lost, why they'd lose again or anyone else would lose if it happened all over again."

I started to run again, past the far side of the Great Room into the storage area. In the dim light, I ran along the room's length, past the rows of shelves and the provisions there, the ammunition, the spare parts, the clothes, stopping by a small niche in the wall, a steel tool cabinet there.

I threw my body against the tool cabinet, nudging it aside, then shifted it away from the wall. There was a steel door, three feet square, a combination lock on it. I twirled the dial on the lock, twisted the handle, the door swung.

I found a flashlight and unscrewed the butt cap, dropping in two D cell batteries. I turned back to the shelves. From a box I took an American flag and returned to the escape tunnel and started to crawl toward the first rung.

My feet inside, I closed and sealed the door. I stopped before a second door, identical to the first. Once on the other side, I sealed it also and soon a third door and sealed it behind me.

I reached the final door handle, above me, the sky rumbled with thunderclaps, massive, unimaginably huge lightning bolts cutting through the clouds, ball lightning rolling from horizon to horizon as I shouldered myself out of the escape tunnel.

I crouched beside the opening at the top of the mountain. In the distance, I could see one of the Soviet helicopters crashing down, struck by the lightning, burning. One remained.

I ran crouched, toward the center of the mountaintop. My radio aerial was camouflaged in a bracken of scrub pine. I reached for the antenna mast, electricity sparking from it and I drew back.

A strong wind whipped across the mountain top as I secured the grommets on the flag to the antenna mast, the flag catching in the stiff wind, unfurling, blowing across the top of the mountain. I stepped back, staring out across the valley.

Thunder came in waves as lightning bolts ripped the sky. Out of the black sky, the last Soviet helicopter came firing its machineguns, the rocks around my feet chipping up, seeming to explode. I ran for the escape hatch.

A missile launched from the gunship, a smoking trail, exploding less than a dozen yards from the blowing flag. I hit the ground, the concussion stunned me. The flag was ripped, tattered, but still there. The Soviet helicopter was making a run, coming low, its coaxially mounted machineguns blazing, slugs impacting around the flag.

"No-o-o!" I screamed the word, my hands flashing up to the twin stainless Detonics .45s, ripping them from the leather.

On the horizon, the sky was burning, like a wave, the fire licking across the air, toward me, engulfing the ground. I could see inside the cockpit of the chopper, past the open cockpit door.

"Rozhdestvenskiy!"

Chips of the rock floor beneath me, chewed up under the impact of the machinegun slugs... a small wound opening on my left forearm as a rock chip impacted against it. I stood unflinching, the pistols in my hands as the helicopter closed.

Rozhdestvenskiy was leaning out the cockpit door, a submachine gun in his hands, firing.

I shoved both Detonics .45s ahead at arm's length firing first the right pistol, then the left, then the right, then the left...

The helicopter was still coming. The slide locked back on the pistol in my right hand, empty. I shouted, "God Bless America!"

The pistol in my left hand discharged, Rozhdestvenskiy's body lurching, twisting, the submachine gun in the KGB colonel's hands firing still, but into the helicopter.

The fire in the sky was rumbling toward me as I started running toward the open hatch of the escape tunnel. I dove for the tunnel; the fire welled up and consumed the mountain, as it had the sky and the earth below...

E PILOGUE

It is late at night as I finish this. Except for the light of the computer
screen, the house is dark and still. I sit alone... no that is not correct... I sit by
myself as the ghosts and memories of this story walk around me... calling to
me. Sometimes, the faces... I have forgotten their names. Sometimes the
names no longer have faces.

Why did the Rourkes survive? Why did we escape the bombs, the ruined
towns? Why did fathers and mothers and husbands and wives and infant
children die and we survived? Short answer... John Thomas Rourke. Had it
not been for him, I would not have lasted two days. Long answer... well, I am
still working on that. What I can say is that having survived, I do have the
chance to be "better."

I have the chance to fulfill a purpose, even though I am not sure what it is.
How do I feel about surviving? Glad I did, sorry others did not... Certainly
there were many others that deserved to survive more than I did. Why then
me? The psychologists call it Survivor's Guilt. I call it hell.

Here's what I do know, we survived when others did not. I think it is up to
us to create our own reason for survival. I think we have and we continue to.
But what about the dead... so many...

I remember John telling me once, the Greeks had a belief that if the living
spoke the name of the dead and spilled wine... for that moment... for that
instant, the dead were alive and would never be forgotten.

Smiling, I rub my face vigorously with both hands. I push back from the
desk and go to the kitchen and open the cupboard. I find a small glass, the

bottle of Seagram's and behind it a small wooden box that was a gift from John Rourke.

I carry all three outside and set them down at the patio table. The night is fresh; a warm breeze is blowing toward the ocean carrying the scent of tropical flowers out to sea. There are more stars in the sky than a man could count in several life times. And there... a shooting star going across the sky from left to right.

I pour three fingers of Seagram's in the glass and from the box I pull one of John's long thin dark cigars and a box of old Strike Anywhere matches. Striking the match with my thumbnail, a trick John taught me, I remember how once the sulfur ignited under my thumbnail. Hurt like hell and healed slowly.

I let the sulfur burn completely away before touching the flame to the cigar. A couple of puffs and it burns nicely. Smoking was not a habit I had picked back up, but on a night like this one... dropping the match into the ash tray, I take another puff and sit quietly.

I swirl a sip of the Seagram's around in my mouth before swallowing and softly say, "To the world we knew," and pour a measure of the whiskey on the grass next to my chair.

After several more puffs and more than a few sips... a bit of time goes by before I softly add, "To the world we now have."

I take another sip and look at the stars before checking my watch and smiling. I pour another glass of whiskey and light another cigar and wait for the dawn.

A dawn that will not bring flames.

On Sale Now!

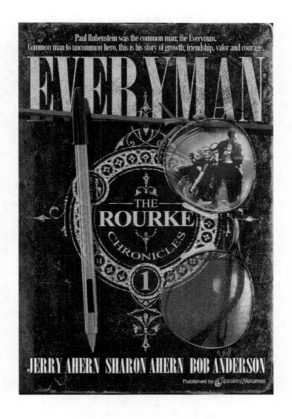

For more information
visit: www.speakingvolumes.us

On Sale Now!

The Survivalist series

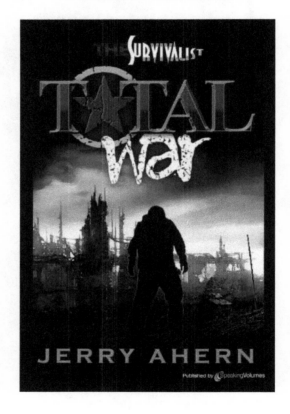

For more information
visit: www.speakingvolumes.us

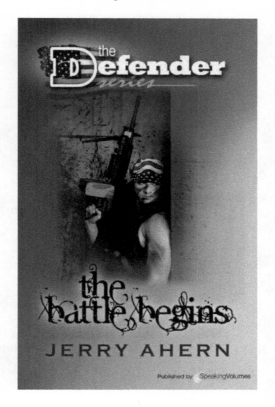

On Sale Now!

TAC Leader series

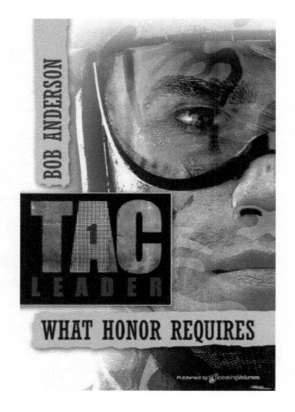

**For more information
visit:** www.speakingvolumes.us

On Sale Now!

For more information
visit: www.speakingvolumes.us

CPSIA information can be obtained
at www.ICGtesting.com
Printed in the USA
LVHW030609301118
598764LV00001B/310/P